palfi
WAYNE

Wayne, Teddy, author
Apartment
33410017163215   06-30-2021

APARTMENT

APARTMENT

TEDDY WAYNE

THORNDIKE PRESS
A part of Gale, a Cengage Company

LIBRARY OF CONGRESS CIP DATA ON FILE.
CATALOGUING IN PUBLICATION FOR THIS BOOK
IS AVAILABLE FROM THE LIBRARY OF CONGRESS

ISBN-13: 978-1-4328-7997-6 (hardcover alk. paper)

Published in 2020 by arrangement with Bloomsbury Publishing Inc.

Printed in Mexico
Print Number: 01   Print Year: 2020

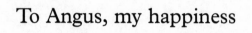

To Angus, my happiness

Incapable of living with people,
of speaking. Complete immersion in
myself, thinking of myself. Apathetic,
witless, fearful. I have nothing to say
to anyone — never.

— Franz Kafka, diary entry,
April 27, 1915

The happiness of being with people.

— Franz Kafka, diary entry,
February 2, 1922

■ ■ ■ ■

1996

■ ■ ■ ■

1

I was looking down at my lap, wishing I weren't there, when I heard Billy speak for the first time.

"I guess I had a different take from everyone else," he said in a baritone as flat as the Illinois topography from which it came.

I couldn't see him, as we were at opposite ends of a classroom, its windows wide open to alleviate the torpor of late August 1996. Should previous decades be defined by an article of clothing and an intoxicant — a gray flannel suit and a martini, tie-dye and marijuana, bell-bottoms and hallucinogens, shoulder pads and cocaine — the mid-nineties were relaxed-fit Gap jeans and light beer. An edgeless era of global-superpower peace and American prosperity, sandwiched between the triumphant and calamitous falls of the Berlin Wall and the World Trade Center. The outcome of the most inconsequential presidential election of modern times, Clinton-Dole, surprised no one. The interregnum for mindless and all-consuming scandal, a year removed from the double murder trial of a football player turned movie star, seventeen months from the revelation of Oval Office fellatio. McVeigh, Koresh, Kaczynski, their obverses a brood of floppy-haired matinee idols, each tending to his own private, melancholy wound.

The dozen graduate students in our stuffy Dodge Hall room were part of a much larger cohort enrolled in Columbia University's Master of Fine Arts Writing Program. Our fiction workshop leader for the fall semester, Sylvia, had been garlanded with a general's uniform of awards for her debut novel two decades earlier and had produced just one other since then — "a slender volume" was the tag applied to that one-hundred-forty-page white-space-filled book. Her modest output, however, had only burnished her renown as an author of sparingly curated and therefore ostensibly perfect words, and we first-years were duly awed by her reputation, along with the contrast of her silver hair and fire-engine-red lipstick.

She had called us a few weeks before the semester began, drafting volunteers to bring work to our brief orientation meeting so we would have something to discuss in the opening class. Hoping to impress as an intrepid pioneer, I had signed up and photocopied the first chapter of my novel in progress. In truth, I was terrified of Sylvia's and my peers' judgment. I'd been accepted to Columbia on the strength of my most polished story from my undergraduate days and hadn't shown anyone the four hundred extant pages of *The Copy Chief,* whose setting was inspired by one of the freelance copyediting jobs I'd held in my two postcollegiate years at a glossy men's magazine in Midtown Manhattan.

The narrator of *The Copy Chief* is — shockingly — a young copy editor toiling in a freelance capacity at a glossy men's magazine in Midtown Manhattan. He describes the periodical as "the kind that often photographed its monthly male cover model in a sweat-glazed, post-workout glow, superimposed over which were exclamatory imperatives to its readers to gain grooming, sartorial, and abdominal mastery." In an inspired twist, our introspective hero happens to be writing a novel that no one else has read but that is, it is strongly implied, a work of singular brilliance. He is supervised by a middle-aged copy chief, Bart (an homage to "Bartleby, the Scrivener"), who

13

speaks roughly ten words aloud each day as he pores over the minutiae of the magazine, ensuring there are no grammatical or spelling mistakes and that the indexed listings of hair products are in the proper house style (name, price — never the reverse).

"A good copy editor's presence is barely felt," Bart tells the narrator on his first day. "If you're good, you go unnoticed."

I had, of course, worked under a similar man, though nothing dramatic ever occurred during my tenure. Among other infidelities to autobiography, the protagonist, by the end of the first chapter, finds the scribblings of the copy chief in his wastebasket late one night, discovering that Bart, by day a slave to desiccated language and late-capitalist vacuity, possesses a richly imaginative private life in which he repurposes the magazine copy as enjambed poems. The narrator is heartened that his affectless boss nurtures this hidden passion yet despairs to see the unripened fruits of it rotting away — the minor-key tragedy of suppressed creativity. The rest of the novel tracks him as he unearths embezzlement at the magazine, perpetrated by the caddish editor in chief, and reports on it in a long article published in the magazine itself, thanks to the assistance of Bart, who smuggles in the exposé after hours. Both men are grandly rewarded by the publishing industry for their heroism. I had mapped out all the head-snapping plot points in a spreadsheet, with additional columns labeled SYMBOLS, THEMES, and ULYSSES/ODYSSEY ALLUSIONS.

Two hours earlier, Sylvia, sipping a mug of tea despite the heat, had welcomed us and talked about what she saw as the purpose of workshop. "There is no good reason, at this stage of your life, to play it safe and hold back," she'd said. "This is the time to experiment and make mistakes and open yourself up to brutally honest feedback. That's the only way to grow as an artist. Fail again, fail better."

I was scheduled to be workshopped last of the three students that day, and the dangling threats of brutality and failure didn't help my nerves. The first writer up was a girl with a delicate voice that sounded on the verge of breaking as she read a page from her story, about a preteen visiting her grandmother's retirement home.

"I really admired how Olivia inhabits the child's point of view in a way that feels authentic" was my only comment, a remark offered as much out of genuine conviction as reassurance for the author's potentially fragile ego. Sylvia and the rest of the class were equally gentle and encouraging, acting less like warriors on the savage rhetorical battlefield MFA classrooms were fabled to be than kindergarten teachers praising a child's first finger painting.

I strained to find something positive to say about the next story but dug deep into my tool kit of workshop jargon. "I have to admit, I initially balked at the spaceship setting," I said, "but I thought Jacob defamiliarized it with such deft prose." The class was again in genial agreement, the tenor that of a mutually supportive group therapy session.

"As I read *The Copy Chief,* I had a few questions," Sylvia said, her reading glasses beginning their perpetual slippage down the slope of her Roman nose. "Namely, is the choice of a writer-protagonist in a bildungsroman too facile and predictable? Don't we assume from the outset that, despite the obstacles in his way, he'll eventually come into his own as an artist, as the genre essentially mandates?"

Her sentences were incontrovertible declarations of fact masquerading as inquiries. Though she issued a follow-up hedge — "Of course, that may be the author's desire, to portray a writer struggling under the weight of his own clichés" — Sylvia's opening remark had the effect of adding a drop of blood to shark-infested waters.

"The literary references felt overdetermined," a student said. "The main character's not really someone I want to root for," said another. And the most lacerating dig: "He comes off like an upper-middle-class whiner."

My classmate exposed an insecurity that had burrowed deeper in recent years as the gaudy excesses of the eighties had backlashed into a post–Cold War fetishization of authenticity: the obvious socioeconomic advantages of my accurately pegged provenance nonwithstanding, it was a severe artistic drawback. A sturdy, dull rung on the tax ladder, not wealthy enough to salaciously spy on the true upper crust, too cosseted to send back dispatches on the destitute, and not even in the broad middle swath of America, where every adolescent experience, every chili dog eaten, every keg party in the woods, could feasibly represent some neo-Rockwellian universal. Probably half of our incoming class had had a similar upbringing — Columbia's extortionate tuition and dearth of fellowship stipends saw to that — but I nonetheless became the workshop's whipping boy.

The comments grew fanged, cataloging irksome details and turns of phrase, an uncensored focus group for a despised product. Forbidden by protocol to speak, I masochistically transcribed my classmates' slurs in my spiral-bound notebook, though I knew I was done with the novel. Keeping it to myself had let me prolong the fantasy that I was crafting a masterpiece in seclusion. But I wasn't. I was merely another Steve (my real-life inspiration for Bart) in the making, educated well enough to smooth out the choppy syntax of a middle-brow magazine or write a serviceable academic paper yet missing whatever it took to produce real literature — which the fictional Bart had, at least, buried beneath his layers of blank banality.

"You know how book reviews always call something 'unflinching'?" a girl asked. "Well, here it feels like the protagonist *is* flinching, like he doesn't want to really examine himself. And I wonder if all the plotty stuff that's happening is to make up for the fact that this isn't juggling enough emotional balls in the air."

The heat that had been gathering in my body for half an hour broke through the skin like a barbarian horde breaching a walled city, my hairline prickling and my lower back moistening with perspiration. My hyperactive sweat glands have always punched well above their weight class, a condition exacerbated by crowded spaces or, as it was then, observation by others. The dog-days mugginess provided some cover for my secretions but also made it worse, and soon a fat drop of sweat dripped down my nose and plopped onto my notebook, splotching the blue ink into a watercolor; then another, detonating like a compact liquid bomb. I could sense the others noticing and swiped my brow with a forearm. It came off shiny as an eel.

Then Billy spoke.

"It evokes the tedium of office life without being boring itself, which is hard to do," he continued after acknowledging his difference of opinion. "I see how his background could rub people the wrong way, but I thought the narrator was pretty conscious of it. And you can't really help what you're born into."

He paused. "I don't know," he said. "I just really liked it."

Upon hearing this lone, plainspoken but carefully considered voice of dissent, the class appeared as taken aback as I was. My sympathetic nervous system finally ceased its frenetic pumping. After a disoriented silence — no one had the heart, or lack of it, to resume the pile-on — Sylvia declared that class was over, and I gathered everyone's marked-up copies of my chapter and editorial letters to me.

Billy was one of the students who distributed pages for the next week. Before I could glance out of curiosity at his first page, someone suggested we all go for a drink.

Most of the class migrated from Dodge Hall to a characterless bar a couple of blocks away. After our group staked out a corner in a crowd composed mostly of Columbia students, I went to the men's room to splash water on my face. When I returned, my classmates had ordered pitchers of beer and were dividing up to play darts. Billy and I were assigned to the same team.

"Thanks for that, back there," I said quietly.

"No need to thank me," he said.

I hadn't gotten a good look at him up close before. His face was framed by black hair that fell in low-amplitude waves to his jaw, at which point its ends curled up like old parchment. He wore a faded and holey black T-shirt of gauzy cotton, the kind I always foraged for in East Village vintage stores, both for their appearance and because, counterintuitively, their semi-sheer material masked sweat well. They couldn't be acquired new but had to have the right original constitution then be worn down over hundreds of wearings and washings while still preserving their basic integrity. His jeans, though, were acid-washed and tight, a stylistic decade behind everyone else's, and came up an inch or two shy of where they should have dropped — which only called attention to his equally unfashionable sneakers, a dirty pair of white LA Gear high-tops with powder-blue accents. From the waist up, he fitted in; below, he resembled a Times Square tourist.

Most of my classmates were around my age, with a few late bloomers in their thirties and forties. The younger ones struck austere poses with their cigarettes, signifying fierce intellect and tormented inner lives, but on the whole they were an earnest-looking lot. The name, rank, and serial number of hometowns, colleges, and previous jobs were referenced. When it was my turn to address the entire group, I did so with the ungainliness of a passenger climbing the first steps of a stalled escalator. Billy said he was from a small town in Illinois no one would have heard of and that he "went to school out there" and had been bartending before coming to New York.

Our teammates proved competent on their first turns at darts, both hitting targets two out of three throws. The next time we were up, Billy deferred to me. I'd hardly ever played before. Holding my beer mug in one hand to feign nonchalance, I aimed repeatedly, like an anxious pool shooter retracting his cue too many times. My first throw veered right of the dartboard, striking the pockmarked wooden wall and clattering to the floor. I overcorrected for the second. My last split the difference — the Third Way, in the political parlance of the time — but clanked unluckily against the metal frame on the dartboard's circumference before it, too, fluttered downward like a gun-shot bird. I stooped to pick up the three fallen arrows, all those gym-class mortifications rushing back.

"I'm just lulling the other team into a false sense of security," I told Billy when I returned. "Setting them up for you."

"Like Newman and Cruise in *The Color of Money*," he said.

"Never saw it."

"It's good," he said. "Not as good as *The Hustler*, but good."

When it was his turn, he, too, held his beer in one hand, cigarette suspended from his lips, and squared up with two practice align-ments, calmly and precisely, like a seam-stress threading a needle. The dart landed in one of the numbers we needed, as did his second attempt. He took extra time on his last throw, which hit the outer ring of the bull's-eye. Our teammates clapped. Without any grandstanding he plucked out his shots, tallied up his score on the chalkboard, and handed the darts to the next player.

"The ringer," the guy said in that admir-ing but still authoritative voice men employ when paying respects to other men's supe-rior achievements.

"I'm not sure that's a good thing," Billy said.

Our team ended up winning, thanks in large part to his prowess, and the game disbanded as the alcohol lubricated conver-sation. While I waited at the bar to order another drink, Billy approached. "Hey, man," he said. "What're you drinking?"

"Haven't ordered yet," I said. "Whatever you're getting."

Billy made eye contact with the bartender. "Two whiskeys, neat, please," he said.

A strong scent from Billy's body overpow-ered the bar's fried finger food and spilled beer. The primary layer was the smoker's tobacco aura, but under that lurked the nautical astringency of Old Spice deodorant, which I had long associated with my father.

The bartender served us, and I paid before Billy could take out his wallet. "For the workshop defense," I said.

"I got the next one," he said. "And you deserved better than that. If you want to show me the next chapter . . ."

"Thanks. But after that, I'm not sure it's worth it."

His wasn't the kind of smile that lights up a room, with its implications of shotgun-spray incandescence, a movie star's or senator's weaponized charm. The bottom teeth were an unruly trap of dungeon spikes, though the top were straight, with one of the central incisors slightly chipped. But, detectable even then, it communicated something subtler: that he and the recipient alone shared a tragicomic appreciation of the world. Life didn't always work out the way we wanted it to, it seemed to say, but perhaps that was the point of it.

"I read an interview with some writer who said whenever he finishes a book, he puts it in a drawer for six months before he looks at it again," Billy said. "And then he sees all the problems with it he couldn't see before."

"Maybe I'll do that," I said. "In six years."

We raised our drinks. He slugged his back despite its not being in a shot glass, and I did the same, though I'd never been much of a whiskey drinker. He ordered two more, this time on the rocks, and paid. We drank at a more sedate pace and lit fresh cigarettes.

"And you're from Illinois and went to college out there, you said?" I asked after I'd told Billy my Massachusetts hometown was twenty minutes from Boston.

He hesitated, his tongue caressing the slant of the chipped tooth. "To be honest, it was a community college," he said. "I applied to a bunch of MFA programs and hoped they'd accept me even though I didn't go to a four-year. Sylvia's the only one who let me in."

I nodded.

"Maybe don't mention it to the group?" he asked. "I don't want anyone wondering if I pulled strings or something to get in."

"Yeah, of course."

After another beat, he chuckled. "Why am I bullshitting? I just don't want them knowing I went to community college."

"Don't be silly," I said. "Everyone knows the MFA application is based almost entirely on your writing sample. And besides, that's something to be proud of — going from community college to an Ivy League grad school." My intended compliment echoed cringingly. "I didn't mean it to sound like that. It's impressive that you've managed —"

"It's cool," he said. "I'm your classic rags-to-rags tale."

To get off the subject, I asked if he was in university housing in Morningside Heights, like most grad students, but he said he was in the East Village.

"Where exactly?"

"Near this bar I work at, the Eagle's Nest? It's on Tenth Street and First Avenue."

"I'm over in Stuy Town," I said.

"Stuy Town? So not in New York City?"

"It's not an actual town," I clarified. "Stuyvesant Town is a residential development just northeast of the East Village. It's huge. Something like a hundred apartment buildings."

"How long you been there?"

"Since freshman year of college. It's technically my great-aunt's." I gave the sheepish smile I always did when revealing the next part. "The apartments are all rent-stabilized. I'm subletting sort of illegally."

The longer version was that Stuy Town, despite being situated in an otherwise nameless neighborhood abutting the East Village and posh Gramercy Park, had a years-long wait list for its rent-stabilized apartments. My great-aunt had maintained a two-bedroom unit since 1970 but left it for her new male companion's New Jersey home the year I matriculated at NYU. My father, divorced and the sole sponsor of my education on his chemical engineer's salary, asked her if I could live there to spare him the university's costly room and board. Many tenants profitably and illicitly sublet under penalty of eviction, but she consented, provided he reimbursed her for the rent and I didn't take in a roommate, which would multiply my chances of getting caught; she wanted to hold on to her lease in case things didn't pan out across the Hudson River.

And so, as college began, rather than receiving keys to a bunk-bedded dorm room, I was handed a set for a two-bedroom apartment of my own. My great-aunt's relationship took, and ever since, to elude discovery from Stuy Town management, I'd kept a ghostly, skulking profile, never hosting any parties and avoiding elevator talk with my neighbors.

"So the landlord can kick you out if he finds out you're living there?" Billy asked.

"It's a management company, not a single person, but yes — though that should change soon." I explained the loophole I'd learned about only that spring. A realtor at a party informed me that under New York City law, we could transfer the lease if I established cohabitation with my great-aunt for twelve months; a utility bill under my name would suffice. As my great-aunt planned by then to live out the rest of her days in New Jersey, she was fine with ceding ownership, and in June I doubled down on my real estate chicanery by registering the phone bill in my name. By the next summer, with this spurious claim of co-residency, I would be able to lay legal and permanent claim to one of the most sought-after possessions in cutthroat Manhattan: rent-stabilized housing, a powerful advantage in launching a career in the arts.

I didn't mention how cheap my rent was, nor that it was an embarrassment of square footage, nor that my father, encouraged that I was taking a foal's first shaky steps toward My Gainfully Employed Future by attending Columbia, had generously offered to pay not only the tuition but also my rent and living expenses for the two years I was in school, a stimulus package I accepted with more guilt than I had as an undergraduate.

"That sounds worth keeping," Billy said. "Rents here are insane."

"It's a pretty run-down apartment, but I'm lucky to have it," I said, a variation on my standard disclaimer.

We were interrupted by a guy in a FREE MUMIA shirt who asked if we were Columbia grad students. When we told him we were, he handed us each a flyer. "We're trying to start a union," he said. "First meeting's next week."

"Think you'll go?" Billy asked after he left.

"I think it's probably more for PhDs than MFAs, since they have to teach," I said, laying the flyer on the bar. "I'm not really much of a joiner, anyway. I never signed up for a single extracurricular activity in school."

"Me neither, except the basketball team." He checked his digital watch. "Shit, gotta go to work. See you next week."

He finished off his drink and left without saying goodbye to anyone else. I melted into the remaining clutch of writers.

"How far into your novel are you?" asked Olivia, the girl who had gone first in workshop.

"Only that chapter," I lied. "But based on today's enthusiastic feedback, it seems like I should turn it into a five-hundred-page epic."

An anxious look flickered across her face.

"I'm kidding," I told her. "It clearly didn't go over well. I'll 'fail better' next time."

"Aw," she said sympathetically, if unconvincingly.

I hovered, as was my style in any group setting, at the periphery, talking to the other strays. As with my extracurricular nonparticipation, I had been a historical interloper who resided on the borders of several crowds, never fully inhabiting them, voluntarily or not. "Floater" would be the term of flattery, connoting nimble social skills and a chameleonic ability to blend in, though I wasn't nearly that smooth. I could generally hold up my end of a conversation, knew how to listen and make jokes, but it was a performance, canny mimicry of how I had seen others interact: you nod agreeably at this moment, you supply your opinion or anecdote or question at this juncture, you make a concerned face (*aw*) over this unpleasant revelation. I rarely allowed myself the easy way out through what I thought of as "script reading," consistently reciting the same breezy phrase for greetings or farewells, or recycling an impression or story verbatim. I wasn't talk-show-host suave, nor was I awkward or robotic; the seams were well hidden, and the end result was apparent normalcy. Only I was aware of how much effort went into making it look effortless.

Living in Stuy Town rather than the NYU dorms hadn't helped matters in college. I'd missed out on much of the proximally convenient freshman-year friendships, the casual hallway encounters at midnight that evolve into four-hour conversations. Then not having a regular office job after graduation pushed me further to the outskirts of my various spheres; co-workers were in my life for a week or two before I moved on to the next temp gig, often not long enough for them to learn my name. I made individual friends along the way with whom I had dinners, gossiped over drinks, tagged along on group outings. But over the previous six years, I'd spent more time alone in my living quarters than anyone my age that I knew of, and my social muscles had atrophied.

A classmate in the bar launched into a story about seeing a mouse in her apartment, buying a humane trap because she couldn't bear to kill it, then going away for a weekend and returning to find the mouse's corpse in the trap after it had starved in confinement over forty-eight hours, the most inhumane death possible. This led to others sharing their narratives of pests and infestations. My habitual discomfort with

31

claiming the spotlight kept me quiet, but I told myself that this was the kind of mundane cowardice that reinforced my distance from people, that the longer I hid behind a lead apron of silence, the harder it would be to shed it, that I was twenty-four years old, for God's sake, and something this small shouldn't be so agonizing.

When there was a gap in the banter, I forced myself to step into it.

"I came back to my apartment after a week away this summer." All eyes turned to me; my heart quickened. "And hundreds of ants were crawling around an open bag of sugar in my cupboard." There were appreciative expressions of disgust.

"What'd you do?" Jacob asked.

I hadn't told this story before and didn't have a punch line ready, largely because, I realized only then, there wasn't much of a story: I had just spent an hour killing them.

"They're paying rent now," I said. "So it all worked out."

The others laughed, I felt relief, and a scruffy guy named Kevin regaled us with an account of the time a "huge mother-fucking raccoon" had chased him down a Memphis street and onto the hood of a car. The details were funny, but his delivery was what really had us all hooked; he was a natural raconteur, pausing dramatically, slipping into outlandish voices, and addressing seven strangers as comfortably as if he were in a tête-à-tête with a longtime friend.

I used to be inspired by people like him, thinking that, with practice, I could attain that kind of ease. But the older I got, the more I was convinced it was something you were born with.

On the downtown 9 train I read Billy's workshop submission, the first chapter of a novel called *No Man's Land.* It was single-spaced, in ten-point Courier font with skinny margins. The narrator was a middle-aged, underemployed, unnamed mechanic, divorced after the death of a young son, living in an economically depressed small Midwestern town I took to be a stand-in for Billy's. The story concerned his quest to resuscitate the engine of a 1967 Chevy Impala his recently deceased father had bequeathed him, but it was mostly a pretext for him to ruminate about the internal workings of cars, the weather, and once-vibrant businesses and establishments that were now gone.

In synopsis, it could come off as a pretentious snooze, but I found myself underlining and checkmarking nearly all the sentences, stark and Spartan but shot through with painterly metaphors and images. *No Man's Land* was what I wished my over-stuffed fiasco of a New York City novel served up in slick magazinese had been: a streamlined narrative, delivered with a brute lyricism, that zeroed in on the mind of a man in a flyspeck of a town. It fell under the film critic Manny Farber's rubric of "termite art," a small-canvas work that methodically eats at its own borders, saying more in its straitjacketed space than a bloated saga ever could with its boldfaced Important Themes. Billy had the quiet confidence to write a novel without the peacocking strut of so many first-time novelists — especially young men hungry to prove themselves worthy of a seat at the canonical table.

I can't remember his words from that first draft, now lost at sea. I recall only that I read with the fervor that I had felt discovering literature in my early teenage years but that had eroded over time with age and academic specialization. By the time I finished, the train was coasting into Houston Street, two stations past my transfer at Fourteenth. I didn't mind; I had come upon an uncommon literary talent, and any jealousy I might have had over a classmate's preeminence was allayed by Billy's modesty and generosity. I got the feeling he didn't understand just how good he was.

When I emerged from the L into the cool, charcoal evening on First Avenue, by the Papaya Dog and discount pizzerias, I didn't want the night to end. I strolled into Stuy Town through its Fourteenth Street southern entrance and walked east through the complex's dense forest of nearly identical redbrick buildings harboring tens of thousands of residents, meandering along its internal service roads and paved walkways, past the playgrounds, the grassy spaces, the basketball courts, and the fountain surrounded by a large cement oval ringed with benches. I made it all the way to its border at Avenue C, clamorous with the whoosh of freeway traffic on the FDR Drive, surveyed beyond it the calm East River, on whose floor rested, in my tabloid-fed imagination, scads of anchored corpses, crossed Twentieth Street into adjoining (and carbon-copied) Peter Cooper Village, headed up to its northern edge at Twenty-Third, and finally turned around for my building on the southeast corner of Twentieth Street and First Avenue.

It was hot as always when I stepped inside my door. Air-conditioning would have necessitated rewiring the unit and drastically raising the utilities-included rent, so I lived without it. In July and August the eighth floor seemed to collect the humidity of all five boroughs, and in winter the building-controlled radiators hissed and rattled incessantly as a safeguard from pneumonia for the complex's many senior citizens, who clung to their bargain apartments till death.

I filled a glass with tepid water from the kitchen's cavernous two-basin sink and knocked out some ice cubes from the tray in the ancient freezer, which contained an interior metal box that developed a sheath of ice around its walls. Every few months I had to chip away at this layer with a knife, dislodging thick chunks with a satisfying glacial calving. (Even more gratifying: the second step of melting holes into a plank of ice under a stream of scalding water.)

I took my drink into the living room, whose furnishings and curios were all my great-aunt's. A deceptively comfortable couch, whose nubby upholstery was scabbing off as if afflicted with leprosy, was parked against a wall; near the entrance, a low-slung marble table supported a wooden console housing a cassette player and phonograph; scores of blue and green glass bottles that she had inexplicably collected over the years lined the bookshelves; and the pièce de résistance: a vintage green-leather-topped mahogany desk with brass handles that presided over it all like an imperious CEO. A skin of silty dust begrimed nearly every surface, the by-product of leaving the windows open every season but fall.

I sat down on the covered radiator to review my classmates' editorial letters and line edits of *The Copy Chief,* ashing a cigarette out the window. Uptown, the Empire State Building was illuminated in blue and white. Below was a workaday block with a Gristedes supermarket, a nondescript women's clothing store whose facade and fashions predated the sexual revolution, a bodega, a serviceable Thai hole-in-the-wall. An ambulance howled up the avenue, a regular occurrence given Stuy Town's location among a cluster of hospitals. The grist for life's mill, the pedestrian tableau always indicated, existed elsewhere, but its very blandness supplied a legitimacy unavailable to the rest of the island — a New York without pretensions of grandeur or grit, absent the hyperbole promised by fictional and cinematic depictions. Smoking by the window as an undergrad in the self-conscious posture of the artist-observer had amplified this sensation, made me feel a member of the genus that had broodingly done the same for decades and found connection, in some intangibly tendriled way, to the city from their cooped-up aeries, and not just a child of the Boston suburbs who had lucked into a steal through a relative.

Except this night, after I'd read *No Man's Land,* Manhattan no longer presented itself to me as the profoundest wellspring of literary material. Billy's anonymous Midwestern town, with its flat, forlorn landscape and dilapidated houses and boarded-up storefronts, was where, despite all appearances to the contrary, real life pulsed and throbbed. That truly was the Heartland; New York was a flashy but disposable extremity.

After reading Sylvia's comments — she was only a little less harsh on paper than she'd been in the classroom — I found Billy's copy of my chapter. The sentences were slashed with cross-outs and suggestions and the pages littered with much more marginalia than those from my classmates. In almost schoolgirlishly fastidious penmanship, he had written his comprehensive remarks in the white space of the last page, where he praised the chapter as fulsomely as he had in workshop. I hadn't exactly forgotten Sylvia's appraisal and the hatcheting that had followed, but Billy's note and the scrupulous attention he'd devoted to my work stanched some of the bleeding. He was a serious, gifted writer, and he, if no one else, was telling me I had potential. Maybe it hadn't flowered in *The Copy Chief,* but it would somewhere else.

On the back of the last page he'd written in a different color pen, clearly during the workshop: "P.S. Don't listen to the others — this has enough 'emotional balls in the air,' whatever the hell that means."

I shuffled the dozen copies of my chapter into a neat pile and consigned *The Copy Chief* to the bottom drawer of my desk.

2

The next week we workshopped Billy's novel excerpt. Sylvia again made her imprimatur early, declaring that his portrayal of a mechanic was "without a trace of sentimentality or condescension." Everyone else raved in lockstep about his insider's depiction of the Midwestern working class; "gritty," "raw," and "earthy" were used in three successive comments.

"I read *No Man's Land* as the self-portrait of a man whose identity is inscribed by loss," I said as the conversation was winding down, essentially reciting what I'd written in my editorial letter. "His town, as an extension of himself, is decaying. His work has dried up. Words have replaced engine parts for him as objects to manipulate, so that he can feel useful again. The title can be read as a metaphor for the gradual disappearance and disempowerment of men like him in these forgotten parts of the country."

It was the first time I'd spoken in class since my skewering. Everyone was looking at me except Billy, who was diligently jotting down notes, as he'd done throughout.

"But I think a more compelling interpretation is as the erasure of his patrilineal bloodline," I went on. "His ties to past and future male family members have been severed through the deaths of his father and his son. He has no living male ancestors or descendants to carry on his legacy. He's in a biological 'no man's land.' "

"Wait, he has a dead son?" Jacob asked. "Am I the only one who missed that?" He wasn't, going by the murmurs around the room.

"I think it's lightly hinted at in a few places," I said, unsure of my reading and glancing at Billy for confirmation, but he remained poker-faced.

"But for something that big, wouldn't he be thinking about it *all* the time?" Jacob asked.

"Maybe, but the narration doesn't have to reflect that."

"But the narration *is* his thoughts. It's in the first person."

"Not necessarily," I said, digging in, though now I was convinced by the doubtful faces around me that I was wrong. "The narration is what he chooses to give voice to, to either an imaginary audience or himself. The thoughts about his son are too painful for him to surface."

No one seemed to buy it, and I let it go. We all adjourned to the bar after class and again resorted to darts to compensate for our unfamiliarity.

"Hey, man," Billy said to me at the bar between games. "You didn't have to say all that in class just because of what I said about your book last week."

"I meant it," I told him.

He paid for his whiskey. "Fuck," he said, frowning. "I'm really hemorrhaging money in New York."

"You basically lose ten bucks when you step outside here." I'd expressed many world-weary sentiments on the subject in my time in the city, and my feelings of rent-stabilized fraudulence had compounded since my father had decided to fund my life-style at Columbia.

His watch beeped, and he said he had to get to work. He downed his whiskey, setting it on the bar and wiping up a few drops with the hem of his shirt.

"I'll leave with you," I said. "Same subway stop."

The 9 train arrived at 110th Street as we

pumped our tokens into the turnstiles. We sprinted to the doors, Billy in front. Stimulated by the action — it was hard to say the last time I'd run anywhere — I leaped as I crossed the threshold and smacked the crown of my head on the frame of the subway car. It felt as if someone had conked my skull with a cast-iron skillet.

"Ouch," said Billy, who must have heard the collision and saw me rubbing my head. "You okay?"

I mumbled a yes.

"Indiana Jones, hat-grabbing scene," he said. "New York version."

I nodded but didn't know what he was referring to; I'd seen only the first *Indiana Jones,* once, as a child.

"If you're not sick of talking about your novel," I said once the pain ebbed, "I have some other ideas."

"You're not sick of it yet?"

A man I saw periodically on the subway entered our car, asking for money. He had been burned badly over what appeared to be his entire body, and he wore a hat and sunglasses that partially obscured his face. Billy and I both looked down and stopped talking. As the man passed, Billy dropped a quarter into his cup.

"Just some thoughts that came to me after

43

class," I said after the man disappeared into the next car. "But we don't have to."

He eagerly took his notebook and a pen out of his backpack. His fingers were slender, almost elegant, though his hands looked older than the rest of him. He wrote down everything I said, asking for occasional clarification. I'd been happy before just to be his classmate, to learn from him osmotically, but now I grew excited at what this might blossom into, the sort of close, symbiotic relationship I'd hoped grad school would offer and the Hemingway-Fitzgerald complementary pairing I'd always thought necessary to one's artistic development. I'd never had a mentor, and it was already clear that Sylvia wouldn't fill that role, but a fellow grunt in the trenches might be better.

"Man, I've never heard any of these terms," he said after we transferred to the L and he was reviewing his notes. " 'Intrigants.' 'Embedded exposition.' You really know your shit."

"It's just from other classes," I said. "You know what book yours reminded me of? *Winesburg, Ohio.* You ever read it?"

"Yeah, I liked it a lot."

"Am I right, thinking it was an influence?"

"Huh," he said. "Hadn't thought about that. Maybe subconsciously it got in there."

We reached First Avenue and ascended the stairs. It had gotten dark. Billy thanked me again for my feedback and walked south. I thought about what I might do when I returned to my apartment; I'd had too many drinks to read conscientiously, and nothing watchable was on TV Wednesday nights.

"Hey, maybe I'll grab another drink at your bar," I called after him. "If you don't mind."

"For sure," he said. "But it's a shithole."

"I'm into dives," I said.

A few minutes later we were at the Eagle's Nest. The plain exterior, with just a neon Miller beer sign in the window, gave way to four oxblood vinyl booths, a pool table, and a jukebox playing the quiet opening guitar solo of Led Zeppelin's "Over the Hills and Far Away." The only patrons were two sallow men at the end of the bar, like figures in a Hopper painting, and an elderly man in a herringbone tweed flatcap by himself in a booth, smoking a pipe and reading the *New York Post*. Above the bar sprawled a mural, composed and presented in what I took to be a spirit of East Village irony, of a scowling bald eagle whose talons clutched a rifle crossed with an American flag. Wiping down the counter was a man three decades older than we were, with stringy hair and

45

tomato-colored patches of eczema speckling his face. He tossed the rag under the bar and let himself out through the drawbridge with a wordless nod as Billy slid into his place.

I perched on a stool, pleased with myself to know the bartender in a real dive, not one that was self-congratulatory about its scuzziness. We'd been having whiskey on the rocks at the Columbia bar, so I stuck with it. This was not the kind of establishment that manufactured complicated cocktails, and the taste was growing on me, the pleasure of the esophageal burn that tindered a small hearth in the gut, its warmth blooming outward like a slow-moving stain on a tablecloth.

I took out my wallet after Billy had poured one for me and another for himself. He shook his head and held up his palm, so I placed three singles on the bar for a tip.

"So? Fancy, right?" he asked.

"I like it," I said. "Especially the mural. Very patriotic."

"The owner's a Vietnam vet."

I didn't let on that I'd thought the gun-toting eagle was a joke. "So you plan to work here the whole time you're in school?"

"Maybe," he said. "If I make it. This place is bleeding me dry. And that's even with a full scholarship from Columbia. The copies I made last week for workshop cost me forty bucks."

"It's good you got a scholarship. They don't give many of those."

"There's no way I would've come here if they hadn't. I'm trying not to take out a student loan, but I don't know if I can last any longer."

"I hear you," I said.

"You've got loans?"

I was embarrassed to admit how much easier I had it, and I considered, for a moment, claiming that I was also under financial duress, or at least that I was in hock to my father. But something about Billy — maybe simply his own openness on the matter, and the intuition I had that he was honest at all times, with himself and others — made me feel comfortable telling him the truth.

"My dad's actually paying my tuition," I said. "I think it's his way of compensating for leaving my mom. Over a decade ago."

"Mine left when I was two," he said.

I was glad he'd said that; I related more easily to children of divorce. "Where's he now?" I asked, thinking, from *No Man's Land,* that he might be dead.

"Nebraska."

"He moved for a job?"

Billy laughed. "Any possible way you can scam the government for money and not work, John Campbell has tried it. I haven't talked to him in five years." His tongue probed his inner cheek. "It could be a lot worse. He never hit me or my mom or anything. Just a fucking deadbeat. We're still getting calls from debt collectors."

I drank my whiskey and felt conspicuously upper-middle-class.

"You're an only child?" I asked.

"So far as I know."

"Me too."

"It's weird," he said. "I didn't know any others growing up."

"Same here."

"Your mom had you on the older side?" he asked.

"No, twenty . . . eight."

"So they just didn't want another kid?"

"I think my mom might have."

"But not your dad?"

"I don't really know," I said. "You were saying you're thinking of dropping out?"

He went to top off one of the drinkers and returned.

"Now that I'm at Columbia, I think I could transfer to a school in a cheaper city, where they'd give me a scholarship *and* a stipend," he said. "I'm just getting the degree so I can be a professor someday. It doesn't really matter what school it's from."

"Being here could help you sell your novel," I pointed out. "It might even go for enough money so you don't have to teach."

"Yeah, that'll happen."

"It happens a lot. Look at people like Michael Chabon, Jeffrey Eugenides, Rick Moody. They all have master's degrees. Moody got his at Columbia, in fact. And David Foster Wallace's first book was his *undergrad* thesis, and he published it while he was still in grad school."

"Who's that?"

"David Foster Wallace?" *Infinite Jest* had come out that spring, and if you followed the publishing world at all, it was hard to miss. I'd jammed into a standing-room-only reading by him at KGB Bar earlier in the year and bought a copy but had been daunted by its phone-book heft and novella-thick set of endnotes.

"Should I know him?"

"He writes pretty avant-garde stuff," I said. "He's from Illinois, actually, and he teaches there. You'd like him."

"I don't know many contemporary writers," Billy said. "I'm still sort of catching up."

"Anyway, his last book was a big deal. Maybe yours could be, too. The point is, you never know."

"I think I know pretty well that a novel about a mechanic in the Midwest isn't going to make me a million bucks," Billy said. "But if I can get a steady teaching job, then it doesn't really matter. And I'd rather not be buried in debt when I do it."

That pragmatic approach was how I'd sold the MFA program to my initially skeptical father, telling him, with a heaping of puffery, that most graduates became professors afterward, the next level up in the literary pyramid scheme of writers paying writers to teach them so that they, too, could eventually become the salaried teachers.

"The one thing is that the women here are really beautiful," he said.

"That's true. You have your eye on anyone at Columbia?"

"I don't know. You? Or do you have a girlfriend?"

"No," I said. "I saw a couple girls at orientation. But I don't know if it's the best idea to get involved with anyone in the program."

"Right, don't shit where you eat," he said.

"I also just got out of a two-year relationship."

"It ended because you were coming here?"

"She was willing to move with me. I didn't want her to. She also wanted kids. Within a year or two."

"Wow," I said. "That's young."

"Not where I'm from. Her sister has three kids and she's twenty-eight." He shuddered. "You have any exes in the picture?"

"Not really." I rattled the ice cube against my glass. "I haven't had many long-term things."

"Me neither, except for Alison," he said. "She told me I have a fear of commitment because I'm invisibly damaged."

"Invisibly damaged?"

"It's from a self-help book she read. She was really into them. There was another one she always used for me . . ." He concentrated and snapped his fingers. " 'Concealable stigma.' That one didn't make any sense when she explained it."

"But the other one did?"

"Oh, she was just always saying my dad fucked me up, and I don't let my guard down because I'm afraid to be rejected again, and I don't want to deal with the problem, the usual bullshit." He snorted. "I said, 'Why do you think I'm writing a novel about a guy and his father?' "

"What'd she say?"

"She goes, 'That's not fixing the problem. That's *reveling* in it.' " He smiled over the slew of disclosures. "Shit, man, I'm the bartender. The customer's supposed to be the one spilling his guts. So what's your big issue?"

I swirled my drink and thought about it.

"Fear of commitment from invisible damage," I said.

"It's a universal problem," he said.

One of the other men called for a beer, then a larger group funneled in, and it was some time before he came back.

"Maybe I'll switch to that one," I said, pointing to the middle liquor shelf. "The Laphroaig."

"Hey, do me a favor?" he asked as he poured it. "If I ever mispronounce any words in class, would you tell me?"

"Sure," I said. "Did I screw up the name of the drink?"

"I think it might be *La-froig*," he said. "Not that it matters. But I'm afraid to say anything with three syllables. This is what happens when you get into reading late. And when no one around you does."

"I assumed you were one of those flashlight-under-the-blanket kids."

"Nah, I didn't read a book for pleasure until I was out of high school. And I only started writing the last few years. When'd you get into it?" He laughed at himself. "Jesus. I sound like a ten-year-old on career day at school."

"The summer after seventh grade."

"That's extremely precise," he said. "Or was that when your parents divorced?"

"That wasn't until the next winter, actually. I was just home for the summer without much to do, so I started reading a lot, and by the end of it I decided I wanted to be a writer."

"Just out of boredom?"

"Plus your garden-variety middle school alienation, I guess," I said. "Feeling a little different from the other kids."

He looked at me over the rim of his glass. I was a little uncomfortable in the headlights of his stare and averted my eyes.

"I could never really talk about this stuff with my friends from home," he said.

"Writing?"

"Everything. They're all still into the same puerile shit they were into as kids. The Bears, the Bulls, and the White Sox, playing basketball, video games. I never once told them I was writing a novel."

"What about getting into Columbia?"

"I couldn't hide that," he said. "They asked what MFA stood for, and I told them it was Master of Fine Arts, and they started calling it 'Masturbating Fag Art.'"

"So I take it you're not sending pages back for their edits."

His smile appeared before vanishing just as quickly. "I didn't even let them know when I left."

"Irish goodbye," I said. "I'm a practitioner myself."

"And I'm Scottish," he said.

I brought back pizza for us from a place down the street and refused Billy's reimbursement, as he was still letting me drink for free. I stayed until closing time, the last customer, and asked where his apartment was.

"Well, you could say it's not very far from here."

"What do you mean?"

"I'll show you." He locked the entrance and motioned for me to follow him through a door marked EMPLOYEES ONLY. He yanked a chain, and by the light of a single bulb we groped down a splintery handrail to the basement. "Watch the boxes," Billy said as we slalomed around caches of liquor until we reached another door. He opened it and flicked on a light switch. It was an empty storage room with an air mattress on a rug, a stack of books to its side, and some moving boxes. The space had the moldy odor of a locker room.

"Nice little setup," I said emptily.

"It's more comfortable than it looks," he said. "And surprisingly clean. The owner normally uses it himself as a place to nap. He's letting me stay here till the end of September."

These two rooms seemed to be the entire basement. "Where do you shower?"

"The gym at school."

"And where do you write?"

"I write in a notebook first. Then I put it in my computer" — I hadn't noticed a desktop hiding behind a box — "but I can't plug it in here, so I've been using the lab at school. It's honestly not so bad here. And it's free."

The room did look cleaner than I'd originally thought, but it was still a depressing place to sleep.

"You could crash at my place tonight," I offered.

"Thanks, man," he said. "But I've gotten used to this."

"You sure? You'll get a good night's sleep and your own shower."

"I swear, the mattress is decent. It's probably better than your couch."

"I've got a spare room," I said. "The bed's all made up. It's really not a problem."

He looked at the air mattress. "You sure it's not an imposition?"

I assured him it wasn't. After an indecisive moment, he thanked me and plucked a toothbrush out of a pint glass by the book pile and a pair of boxers, socks, and a T-shirt from one of the moving boxes. There was something heartbreaking not only about the meagerness of his possessions but how neatly stored they were.

He dumped his things into his backpack behind the bar and tended to the final arrangements, placing the night's earnings in an envelope that he delivered to a back room. I'd never had a job that involved a cash register and was impressed with how dexterously he operated it, the smooth ejection of its drawer and scooping up and counting of its different denominations like a manual ballet.

We didn't speak much on the walk home. Upon entering my apartment, he removed his sneakers. "You don't have to do that," I said.

"It's kind of a habit." He placed them under the marble table. "Empire State Building," he said, noticing the view. "Nice.

56

Why's it blue and orange?"

"They light it up for the local teams who win."

"So the Metropolitans of New York actually won a game."

"The Metropolitans?"

"The Mets," he said. "Eddie Murphy in *Coming to America*? 'The Giants of New York took on the Packers of Green Bay'?"

"Oh, yeah," I said.

I showed him to the smaller spare room. He paused in the hallway by the door and examined four framed black-and-white Depression-era photos — North Carolina farmers outside a general store, a busy Harlem block, workingmen at a lunch counter — and read aloud the printed caption to the last one: "Union steward speaking at desk with personnel manager at American Lead Pencil Company."

"Those were all taken by my great-uncle," I told him. "The Works Progress Administration commissioned him to take pictures of people around the country during the Depression."

"So the government just paid him to travel around America, taking pictures?"

"Pretty much," I said. "Not a bad gig."

"He must've been a big deal, for them to do that."

"Not really," I said. "This was the peak of his career. My great-aunt's line is that he never showed his soul in his work, and that's what held him back."

He looked once more at the photo. "Still, that's cool, to have an artist in the family."

"He died when I was three," I said, stepping aside for him to enter the room. The twin bed hadn't been used since an out-of-town college friend had slept over that spring. I gave Billy a fresh towel for the morning.

"Thanks, man," he said. "Appreciate this."

"Don't worry about it," I said.

Normally when I had an overnight guest I felt a faint sense of unease, of someone encroaching upon my space, but I didn't then. When I woke up to the sounds of mid-day traffic, Billy's sneakers were still by the front door. I went out to Ess-a-Bagel on the corner, renowned for its gargantuan pillows of dough, and bought two with cream cheese. Billy was showering when I returned, and I made us coffee in my French press.

"That's some very citrusy shampoo," he said, coming out of the bathroom fully dressed and toweling off his head. "My hair smells like grapefruit."

I held up the paper bag. "Got us bagels

and made coffee."

"Sweet. But I should be treating you."

I ignored it and handed him his bagel.

"Man," he said after taking a bite. "This is so fucking good."

"I know," I said. "I get annoyed when people think the best bagel or pizza place or whatever in New York just happens to be the one in their neighborhood, but these really might be the best."

"I don't have anything to compare it to."

"Well, you just moved here."

He smiled. "This is embarrassing, but I've never had one anywhere. They just opened the first bagel place back home the week I was leaving, and I didn't go," he said. "It was a pretty big fucking deal."

"You haven't even tried one in an airport or something?"

Another smile, this one more uncomfortable. "I'm really coming off like a hick. I've never been on a plane."

"Oh." I chewed my bagel and tried to think of something else to say but couldn't. We ate for a minute in between sips of the coffee. A first sleepover, whether it was sexual or platonic, had a way of making you both more and less comfortable around the other person; you'd jumped a fence of intimacy, but now you saw each other in the blunt morning light.

"Cool desk," he said. "Reminds me of the Oval Office."

Its leather-topped grandeur was embarrassing, signaling a childhood with countless plane rides. "It's my great-aunt's," I said.

He appraised it more thoroughly. "You must feel like a serious writer when you're at it."

"Sometimes, I guess," I said. "Most of the time I feel like a fraud. Like I'm sitting at this big, fancy desk avoiding real work."

"Everyone thinks they're a fraud," he said. "Except for the actual frauds."

Billy might not have known it, but he truly wasn't one. The kind of talent he had was a gift, and not only because of the external rewards it could offer him. It meant that a lifetime of fulfilling work, not just self-doubt, lay ahead. Most people, even those afforded plentiful opportunities through nothing more than good fortune, didn't have that sense of security, the feeling that they were doing exactly what they were supposed to be doing — a calling, not a profession.

"So where are you moving when the bar owner stops letting you stay there?" I asked.

"I'll figure something out," he said.

Whatever he found would be a hovel only marginally better than his basement digs. He would always have to struggle to stay financially afloat not just in New York, but anywhere — and I would always be fine, all because my father was a professional and his was a layabout. I had an abundance of resources; here was a concrete means for me to share it.

But it would be strange to invite him to live with me after knowing him for just a week. And having him around, another body on the radar of management or nosy neighbors, would raise the odds of getting caught. It wasn't worth the risk.

"What're you up today?" he asked as we finished breakfast.

"Dentist appointment," I told him.

After he thanked me and left, there was an odd hollowness in the apartment, an absence I wouldn't have perceived had I not just had a visitor. Once I closed the door to the room he'd slept in the atmosphere returned to normal, and I got ready to leave.

The midtown waiting room was crowded but silent. It was overly air-conditioned, and I shivered as my wrists grazed the metallic arms of the pleather chair. A collection of folk art prints on the wall only emphasized the airport-terminal sterility.

The clinical hush was intermittently punctured by the ding of the elevator door in the hall as new patients arrived. At one point a young couple emerged, the mother pushing a stroller. The father went up to the receptionist. "We're here to see Doctor . . . I'm forgetting his name, the urologist?" he asked.

"Dr. Bloom," she said. "Are you a new patient?"

"It's not for me," he said. "It's for our son."

She handed him a clipboard, and the family retreated to a corner of the room, where the mother breastfed the baby while the father frowned his way through the checklists and questions he never thought he'd have to answer — questions he'd never even thought of. I wondered if my own father had come to my earliest appointments, the ones right after my birth, or if, as he did when I grew older, he'd begged off with work and left it to my mother, who accompanied me to each one until I was able to go to them on my own.

I had two other seminars ("Scenes and Sensibility," "Syntactical Approaches to Prose") and a lecture to read for and attend, so I didn't think much about Billy. That weekend I went to a party thrown by an NYU classmate. The people I knew seemed more impressed with what I was doing with my life now than they'd been the previous two years, when they had expressed a patronizing admiration for my "bravery" in venturing out on my own as a writer. Columbia's graduate program, on the other hand, was a credentialed step in an established system they understood well.

Our workshop went through the same routine that Wednesday: workshop, darts, Billy exiting early to bartend.

"So you're into science fiction?" I asked Jacob, the boy who'd written the spaceship story the first week, after the darts game had wound down.

"Only the good stuff," he said. "Asimov, Heinlein, Dick, Le Guin, those kinds of writers."

I knew nothing about the genre and searched for a related question, or another vein of workshop talk, or something personal but not too personal to ask. But when I came up empty, though there was nothing intimidating or unfriendly about Jacob, the perspiration began.

"Is it hot in here?" I asked.

"Not really," he said.

63

After this, I knew, would be the deluge. Before that could happen I went to the men's room, where I doused my face and neck in cold water and patted a damp paper towel on my lower back. But it was no use; I'd broken the seal, and the sweat had already speckled my heather gray shirt. I'd been through this exact scene countless times — hiding away from others in a bathroom, struggling to dam my pores and make myself presentable. At least the attack the first week of workshop was from an understandable source; a mere lull in conversation had precipitated this one. It was just a minor embarrassment, a bodily glitch many people could easily ignore or joke about, but every time it happened it cemented the feeling I'd had most of my life that no else had this particular problem, there was something off about me, I couldn't even get through an activity as simple as having drinks in a bar with colleagues, I was fundamentally defective.

As I usually did in these cases, I slipped out without speaking to anyone.

After I got out of the subway I paused before heading toward Stuy Town. Billy was four blocks away. It wouldn't be odd to pop in for a quick drink.

"Hey, man," he said when I came into the

Eagle's Nest. No one else was there except for the old man in the tweed cap I'd seen the previous week, still smoking a pipe and reading the *Post* in the same booth.

"Just thought I'd get another drink," I said. "If you don't mind."

He served himself and me well whiskey, deflecting payment again. "For the bagel."

"The bagel was to make up for all the drinks here."

"Then we're square," he said. It was the kind of colloquialism I could never draw on without sounding ridiculous, a mannered aping of dialogue from some seventies film I'd seen.

"By the way, what does 'imitative fallacy' mean?" he asked. "It was in your note about my novel."

"That's the idea that you don't need to make the story or voice exactly like the protagonist," I said. "So it's okay if the average mechanic wouldn't describe the sky with the word 'cerulean,' for instance."

"Or how he wouldn't be thinking openly about his son," Billy said. "You were the only one who caught that. Even Sylvia didn't mention it."

I nodded modestly to mask any smugness.

"And what's that term you used? 'Termite art'?"

"It basically means doing a lot within a narrow frame. Like a termite that's eating away at its boundaries."

He looked thoughtful.

"Or me in my basement room," he said.

The old man cleared his throat and held up a finger. Billy smiled at me, filled a pint glass with Guinness, lopped off the mushrooming head with a silver beer comb, and took it over to the man.

"He was here last time," I whispered under a Springsteen song when Billy returned.

"He's here every single night," Billy said. "Sometimes he falls asleep in the booth, and I have to wake him up at closing time."

The man removed a handkerchief from his interior jacket pocket and dabbed the middle of his foam-licked mustache. He had to be eighty, eighty-five.

"Speaking of your basement room," I said, "I was thinking you could move into my spare room. If you don't have a better option."

His face took on an uncomfortable cast, and I wondered if he thought he'd guilted me into my proposal. "You don't have to offer me your room. I can find a place."

"I know. But it's just sitting there empty. Seems like a waste."

"Don't guests use it?"

"They could sleep on the couch."

"Well, that's nice of you," he said, "but I wouldn't want to cramp your style."

"You'd have your own room, so I don't see how you'd be cramping my style. Honestly, the whole place is too big for just me."

"Your desk is in the living room. I'd be interrupting you all the time."

"I could move it into my bedroom — there's tons of space," I told him. "The spare room's too small for a desk, but we could put one for you in the living room. If you don't mind the distraction."

"I could handle it. But I couldn't afford a place with just one roommate anyway. I'll probably need three or four."

"Oh — I wouldn't make you pay," I said in a tone that suggested I was almost offended by the implication.

"Come on." He cocked his head skeptically. "You wouldn't mind someone — someone you've only known for *two weeks* — living with you for *free*?"

"It's really cheap," I said. "And, actually, my dad's covering the rent while I'm in school."

"But you said you're not there legally?" he asked.

"I'll be legal in June."

"What would happen if we got caught?"

"We'll get locked up in solitary in Rikers," I said. "Really, lots of New Yorkers do this. I've been there six years and I've never had a problem. We just can't have parties."

He sipped his drink and pursed his lips.

"That's very generous," he finally said. "But I'd feel weird not helping with rent. Even if your dad's paying for it."

As I'd tried to convince him, I'd gotten into the idea of having him for a roommate. I could have offered the room to him for a low price within his budget, but I didn't want to render my offer coldly transactional and turn into his landlord, especially when I wasn't paying rent myself.

"How about if you pay me in kind?" I proposed.

"What do you mean?"

"Like doing a few things around the house? Cooking dinner a few times a week, that sort of thing? If you like to cook."

"I'm a decent cook," he said.

"Well, I'm terrible at it and I order takeout all the time, so it'd end up saving me money without costing you anything. Obviously we'd split the groceries."

He considered this addendum to the contract before shaking his head.

"I work here three or four nights a week

and there's a reading at school most weeks, and I make a dinner out of the cheese plate. That leaves only two, three dinners, tops. That's not enough to make up for free rent." He swept peanut fragments from the counter into his palm and chucked them into a garbage can. "What if — never mind, that's stupid."

"What?"

"I don't know. What if I cleaned the apartment?"

He must have noticed the blanket of dust throughout my place and the black grout snaking like ivy around the shower tiles. Cooking was one thing, an activity he enjoyed that helped make a place feel like a home, but cleaning up after me was unmistakably servile.

"I'd feel bad having you do that."

"I actually don't mind cleaning," he said. "I sort of like it, a little. I could do it once a week. That's the only way I'd feel okay not paying you."

"Deal," I said, though it was an odd case of reverse bargaining. "Should we clink glasses or something?"

"I always feel stupid doing that. Let's shake on it."

We did. He looked a little surprised as we made contact, and I suspected he was reacting to the softness of my hands. My excessive perspiration had one benefit, constantly moisturizing my skin, and for years people had told me mine were the softest hands they'd ever touched. When women were the ones to point it out, it was fine, often even flattering — it boded well for the aging process — but I'd always been a little embarrassed when men remarked on it.

He released a burden-venting exhalation and bolted his drink. "Fuck, man. This changes everything. I could actually stay in New York." He looked down at his empty glass. "We can do a little better than this shit."

He wheeled around to the bar and reached for a bottle of Scotch on the top shelf. It was high enough that his shirt rode up his back, exposing a strip of flesh above his jeans.

"I don't know what to say, man," he said as he pulled down the bottle and poured fresh glasses for us. "I really owe you."

"Don't worry about it," I told him.

3

That Saturday afternoon I helped Billy carry everything he owned from the Eagle's Nest to Stuy Town. Beyond a duffel bag of clothes, there wasn't much: a three-drawer metal file cabinet, his already-obsolete beige desktop computer, and a few boxes of miscellaneous items. We got lucky and ran across, on the curb, a rickety wooden desk and a cheap swivel chair, which we transported on the furniture dolly my great-aunt stored in the entryway closet. We moved my leather-topped desk to my bedroom to make space for his and the file cabinet.

While Billy unpacked and organized, I read for workshop on the couch and, at sunset, ordered takeout for us. He came out of his room and stationed a Chock Full o'Nuts can of pens on his desk. "I feel like I've colonized this area," he said.

I was fine with it; for six years the apartment had felt underpopulated, and within a

71

single day it had been filled out as it was meant to be. *"Mi casa,"* I said.

The deliveryman rang up from the lobby intercom. I told Billy I'd ordered Thai food.

"Cool." He took out his wallet. "How much was it?"

"It's on me."

"I thought the whole deal was I'm supposed to cook for us."

"Consider it a housewarming present." I waited for the food at the door to end the argument and divvied up the dishes between two plates.

"I don't have any beer," I called from the kitchen. "Red wine okay?"

"Absolutely not," he said. "Yeah, I drink everything."

As we ate, shouts carried into the apartment from my neighbor, a woman in her eighties who predated my great-aunt in the building. I never saw her outside her unit and only occasionally in the hallway through my peephole. She seemed to spend most of her waking hours haranguing her caretaker and the deliverymen who had the misfortune to be summoned to her door. I'd warned Billy about her before he moved in. We stopped chewing to hear better, though we couldn't make out the specific volley of insults.

"It only gets that loud once in a while," I said. "She shouldn't distract you too much while you're working."

"Man," he said, forking a noodle. "So many tragic lives out there."

"Should we go out and get a drink after this?" I asked, not wanting him to hear the woman all night. "You're not working tonight, are you?"

"For sure," he said. "Anywhere but the Eagle's Nest."

I suggested Chumley's, the former speakeasy in the West Village. "Hemingway and Fitzgerald used to drink there," I mentioned as justification for the trek.

After Billy showered, he asked if I'd noticed that some of the showerhead nozzles didn't work. I told him I tried not to ask my great-aunt to phone Stuy Town's maintenance crew unless it was an emergency, to prevent any questions about why I was the one letting in a repairman.

"Mind if I take a look?"

"Be my guest," I said.

From under his bed he pulled out a tool kit I hadn't seen him move in and opened it in the bathroom. The inside glinted with dozens of implements. "That's a serious tool kit," I said.

"My dad gave it to me when I turned

thirteen. Which is ironic, since he didn't know how to fix shit." He mock-grimaced and made his voice warbly. "And he left us in a broken home." He picked through the kit for a few tools and stood barefoot inside the tub. "You know the last time the showerhead filter was cleaned?"

"I didn't even know there was a filter," I said from the doorway. "So, never."

"Then that's probably the issue. Plus the nozzles get clogged with mineral deposits over time."

He'd yanked the shower curtain all the way to the end, but it was bunched up and blocked my view of his manipulations to the showerhead. All I could see was that he was unscrewing it then wrenching and fiddling with the tools as his left biceps pulsed.

"So who taught you this stuff, if your dad didn't?" I asked.

"I have an older cousin who knows some things," he said. "The rest I picked up by trial and error at home."

"Is that how you know how to fix cars?"

"I don't know anything about fixing cars."

"But . . . your novel."

"Oh," he said. "I just read manuals and change up the words when I need to show the guy doing something. I'm not even that good a driver. I failed my test twice before I got my license."

"No kidding," I said. "It's so detailed. You really fooled everyone in class."

"If anyone else wrote it, they'd assume it was research," he said. "But they think I have, like, motor oil running through my veins."

He removed the showerhead completely and asked if I had a toothbrush I didn't mind getting dirty. I gave him my current one; I'd gone to the dentist before school started for a cleaning and received a new brush. He scrubbed a small plastic object under the sink faucet then brushed the nozzles of the showerhead and asked for a piece of toilet paper, which he used to painstakingly clean between the nozzles. Crumpling the toilet paper into a ball, he arced it like a basketball.

"Jordan!" he said as it sank into the wastebasket. He looked a little embarrassed. "I regress to a fourteen-year-old boy when I throw things out. You a Bird man?"

"What?"

"Larry Bird," he said as he screwed the showerhead back on. "I'm guessing you like the Celtics."

"Oh. I thought you meant am I half-bird, half-man or something." I didn't like the Celtics, had never had any interest in them or their sport despite their run of glory in my youth, but the obsessive fandom of greater New England meant I'd picked up enough data to feign basic comprehension.

"I always thought Bird was better than Magic, except for his back," Billy said as he replaced the filter and showerhead. "But Jordan's in another league."

"Uh-huh," I said.

"I still can't believe Magic came back last year. Can you imagine guarding him, knowing what could happen?"

I nodded.

"I wonder if those rumors about him are true," he said. He stepped out of the tub and turned the faucet. Water streamed out of all the nozzles.

"Nice," I said. "This setup's already paying off."

He opened the medicine cabinet and pointed to a small slot built into the wall. "What's this, by the way?"

"My great-aunt told me it's to deposit used razor blades. I've never used it."

"How do you get them out?"

"You can't."

"They're just stuck in the wall for*ever*?"

I shrugged.

"So when they tear down this apartment, they'll find a bunch of razor blades in the wall from nineteen-whatever?"

"It was built in 1947," I said. "So, yeah, I guess."

"Very cool," he said. "A little time capsule."

He stepped out of the bathroom and, before entering his room, noticed the photo on the wall of the pencil company union representative was askew. When he adjusted it, he discovered the nail holding it was loose. With one clean strike from the hammer in his tool kit, he drove in the nail farther.

"I've been meaning to fix all these loose nails around the place," I said. "But I can't find my hammer."

"Or your sickle," Billy deadpanned.

"I guess that's why communism is dead," I said.

We took the L to the 1 and exited the Christopher Street station to the chaos of its haphazardly intersecting streets and throngs of predominantly male partiers on the prowl. Billy's head whirled around at a drag queen swaggering by on six-inch platforms. On our way to the unmarked venue on Bedford, we passed two men with bulging, gym-acquired muscles.

"Hi, boys," one said.

Billy didn't speak until the next crosswalk.

"So this is obviously a gay neighborhood?"

"Chelsea is the main one. This is a little more mixed," I said. "But the bar's not."

I was relieved when the crowd packed into Chumley's battered wooden booths included plenty of women. We squeezed into an open spot by the bar facing a picture of Samuel Beckett, among other portraits of dead authors and book jackets. The old-timey atmosphere, soaked in soft amber lighting, felt comfortingly permanent. I ordered two whiskeys on my tab, telling Billy it would be easier this way and he could repay me later, though I planned not to remind him of the bill; I liked the idea of treating him on his first night.

"You said Hemingway drank here?" he asked.

"And Fitzgerald," I said. "And Dylan Thomas, and a buncha others."

"Is this, like, a literary crowd, then?"

"Nope," answered the man next to us. He had a thick head of carefully parted white hair and wore a sloppily fitting button-down. "Half these assholes are in finance." He introduced himself as Jim. "This your first time here?" he asked Billy.

"Only mine," Billy answered. "He's been before."

"I've been coming here for thirty-three

years," Jim announced. "The first night was November 22, 1963, the day Kennedy was shot."

"I was here the night of the white Bronco chase," I said. "I'm not joking. Everyone left to watch at a sports bar."

"That's the difference between our generations," said Jim. "JFK for me, O.J. for you."

"Plus you got the moon landing," Billy added.

"Well, we got Crystal Pepsi," I said. "*And* Zima."

Jim smiled thinly and asked what we did. I told him about the Columbia program. "I had a play run off-Broadway in the fall of 1965," he said.

"I've never met a playwright," Billy said.

"Then I got married," Jim went on, "and had kids, and I got a job in life insurance. And I thought I could keep writing at night, or early in the morning, or on weekends, like Wallace Stevens. But guess what I learned?" He waited a beat, though neither of us was going to supply the answer we knew was coming. "It's a hell of a lot easier to write poems in your spare time than plays. Never finished another one again."

"Well, your wife probably appreciated the financial stability," I said.

"*Deeee*-vorced," he said in a singsong voice.

"Or your kids," Billy tried.

Jim shrugged his eyebrows and wavered on his feet; he'd hid his drunkenness before but now evidently didn't care. "I had the beginning of something good, and I stopped," he said. I couldn't tell if he meant his career or a specific play.

"You could always start up again now," Billy said.

"Too late," he said. "I'm out of my time's joint. A real nowhere man. Doesn't have a point of view. No one cares what I have to say anymore."

"Naw," Billy said, doubtless drawing on years of comforting abject drunks at the bar. "You're not a nowhere man. You're still here. We're all still here."

Jim gazed dreamily at the room. "Maybe," he said and, with a hoist of his glass, disappeared into the crowd.

Billy was scribbling in a pocket-sized notepad. "What're you writing?" I asked. " 'Don't get married or have kids'?"

"Sorry, one sec," he said. "Getting down his dialogue." The page he was on was crammed margin to margin with his tidy handwriting.

"That's smart," I said when he was done.

"I never carry around a notepad."

He snapped the notepad shut and replaced it in his pocket. "I try not to take it out in public too much."

"No, it's a good habit," I said.

He looked back at where Jim had gone. "Is this stupid, what we're doing?" he asked.

"We can go somewhere else."

"Not the bar. Getting a writing degree. It's stupid, right?"

"Why? Because of that guy's story?"

He took a long drag on his cigarette, his cheeks caving in, and ejected the smoke through his nostrils like a machine's relief valve. "Maybe I'm just hiding this."

"You're hiding what?" I asked.

"Hiding *in* this," he corrected me; the bar was loud. "From real life and a real job. I'm just bullshitting around in school so I can pretend I'm a writer for a few years."

I'd met aspiring writers as an undergrad who were guilty of what Billy was talking about: ice-cold Didionites, guys who fashioned themselves Bukowski-style misfits or Pynchonesque geniuses or Nabokovian above-it-all aesthetes. One writing student wore a suit and bow tie to all the school readings, where he ostentatiously took notes from the front row in a leather-bound book.

"You're the real deal," I told him.

"Thanks," he said. "Thanks, man. Sometimes I feel like the people at school — including Sylvia — are going easy on me, or kissing my ass. But it means something coming from you. But even if that's true, which is debatable, if I want to make a living, this is the worst possible way to get there."

"It could be worse," I said. "You could be studying poetry." I took the last sip of my whiskey. "Want another round?"

"I was actually thinking we should go home to get some writing in."

"Oh, okay," I said, disappointed at the premature conclusion to the night and wondering why he'd agreed to go all the way to the West Village for just one drink.

"I'm kidding." He grinned slyly. "Let's get hammered."

As I flagged down the bartender, a girl bumped into Billy while maneuvering toward the bar. "I'm so sorry," she said in a British accent, putting a hand on his shoulder.

"That's okay," he mumbled. He attempted to move out of the way, but the space was too tight.

"I can get you a drink," I called over to her.

"I'm actually getting two — one for my friend."

I asked what they were having and ordered for all of us. "So, I imagine you guys want to hang out with us now?" she asked impishly.

Billy and I looked at each other.

"Come on over," she said and walked to the booths.

In my limited experience, when a woman at a bar invited you to sit with her and her friend, you unhesitatingly accepted, but Billy seemed reluctant. "This okay?" I whispered as we threaded through the crowd.

"Yeah," he said.

We joined the two women in their booth, its table a scarified palimpsest of drinkers' names. Naomi, the one from the bar, had a sleek black mane with a Sontagesque streak on one side, Claire's tongue piercing glinted like a wet pebble in the cavern of her mouth, and both were in floral dresses, a trend that had apparently made it across the pond: they were "on holiday" from London.

"Claire writes poetry," Naomi said after I'd answered her question about what we were doing in New York. "That's why we came to this bar."

"Cool," I said. "Have you published anything in America?"

She smiled down at her beer. "Nothing anywhere yet."

"Us neither. At least I haven't. Have you?" I asked Billy, trying to get him involved; he hadn't spoken beyond quietly introducing himself.

"Nope," he answered.

After more conversation about where we all lived and what they'd done on their trip, with hardly a word from Billy, he excused himself to the men's room.

"Can your friend talk?" Naomi asked.

"He's just a little shy around new people," I said, which seemed to be true; he'd been quiet at first with our Columbia classmates and had only lately begun speaking up in class and at the bar after workshop.

"Tell him we're *very* nice."

"I will."

"And tell him," she said, "that I think he's a fucking gorgeous man."

I didn't know why I was the one to blush.

"So," Naomi said when Billy came back, "where can a girl go dancing around here?"

I mentioned a dive with a dance floor near Washington Square Park I'd been to with NYU people. She and Claire stood up. Billy and I stayed seated.

"Coming or not?" Naomi asked. "My God. It's like I have to spell everything out for you two. You Americans aren't much for nuance, are you?"

I closed out my tab and we left with them, Billy and I in front as we smoked in pairs. The night wind carried the first crisp notes of autumn, a season I thought of as one of rebirth rather than death for its school-year associations.

"Naomi's into you," I said under my breath.

"Nah," he said.

"She told me when you were in the bathroom."

"Really? What'd she say?"

I paused.

"I can't remember, but she made it pretty clear," I said.

He glanced backward. "I feel like they can see through me."

"What do you mean?"

"They're from London," he said. "They can tell I'm from the middle of nowhere."

"You live in Manhattan now," I told him. "You're a grad student at Columbia. They're probably intimidated by you."

He arched a dubious eyebrow.

"And no one cares where you're from," I said. "You're here now."

The bar was a dank cave with a loosely delineated dance floor composed of people who resembled us. Young metropolitans in our demographic looked essentially of a piece then, as I suppose they always do, a refined conformity with grace notes of distinction always being au courant — jeans of mildly varying cut and wash, grungy flannels and Cobain cardigans, lanky locks on men, pixie cuts on women, almost to the point of gender convergence, and influenced, respectively, by the early-decade coifs of River Phoenix and Winona Ryder. The guiding tenet was not to look like you spent a lot of money on your appearance nor to look legitimately poor, which called for moderation. It was an unstylish microperiod, best banished to the back of the closet of fashion history, with a potpourri of nineteen-seventies artifacts thrown into the mix — a few bell-bottoms, collars spread like albatross wings, sideburns (Jason Priestley and Luke Perry); cultural nostalgia, so goes the theory, operates in approximately twenty-year cycles, the period required for impressionable teenagers to become adult tastemakers who seek comfort in the rose-colored remembrance of their youth.

I bought vodka shots for everyone, hoping to loosen Billy up, but he remained taciturn.

"I heard you're a great dancer," Naomi said to him after she got the next round.

He permitted a smile small enough that you could barely see his chipped tooth. "Where'd you hear that?"

"Everyone's talking about it," she said. "You want to prove it?"

Billy looked bashful. "I'll go if you go," he said to me.

I signed off, and our quartet migrated to the dance floor. Billy's movements were restrained at first, but I kept plying everyone with drinks, and soon either the alcohol or the release from conversation did the trick for him. He was far from a graceful dancer, however: his motions were jerky, he was consistently offbeat, and his wild gyrations made you worry he might crash into you or elbow your face. Yet for someone who had been insecure about how he fit in, he didn't seem to care how he looked on the dance floor, a more important trait than technical proficiency.

When Oasis's "Don't Look Back in Anger" came on, we paused dancing along with the rest of the crowd, but the entire room sang along to the trifling matter of Sally's waiting — this was all we collectively had, we knew no protest songs, had little to protest — and I felt a swelling in my chest, a surge of joy flowering out through my limbs; there is nothing like crooning in a group to a chorus to communicate to yourselves and the world that you are young and drunk and unhindered by responsibility, that the future stretches out endlessly before you like a California highway.

The swampy air lacquered our skin, mine most of all. My back was soon as drenched as if I'd recently showered, but my undershirt absorbed most of the damage. Billy's gray T-shirt was darkened over the chest and in the armpits. He appeared unaware, or at least unfazed. When the chorus of "Ironic" by Alanis Morissette started, his dancing grew crazier, like a spinning top wobbling out of control. He had to apologize to other people for knocking into them. I grew self-conscious and slowed down to a stilted sway.

Claire did, too. "This isn't a very good song for dancing."

"Isn't it ironic," I said.

"Just because we're on a dance floor and it's not a good dance song doesn't make it ironic," she pointed out. "This song ruined the public's understanding of irony."

"Like how 'rain on your wedding day' isn't ironic. It's just bad luck."

"Exactly."

"But maybe" — I let the suspense build

— "*that's* the ultimate irony of the song."

"That a song called 'Ironic' and is supposedly about various ironies gets the definition of irony wrong." She nodded approvingly. "That's not bad. Did you come up with that?"

"I did," I said. "All by myself."

"And here I was thinking you had nothing inside that head of yours."

"Well, I did play the Scarecrow in my fourth-grade production of *The Wizard of Oz,*" I bantered.

"If you only had a brain," she said — then, with a look of surprised delight as she came up with it, she added, "on your wedding day!"

Claire had dark eyes that looked aqueous when the light caught them, a coy smile through the flirtatious teasing and bad jokes. We had a more natural immediate rapport than I'd had with a woman in a while. Before we could go any further, Billy pulled me by the arm.

"Keep dancing," he commanded, and with his other hand grabbed Naomi, who linked with Claire, who held my hand as we danced in a circle, a sort of "Ring Around the Rosie," and soon I wasn't uncomfortable at all, even when Naomi shouted to Claire, "We're fucking dancing in New York City

89

right now!" because, cringingly overeager sentiment of a tourist though it was, it crystallized the vodka-clear epiphany we were all having: nearly all of one's time is spent not dancing in New York City, is instead wasted on working, on commuting, on shampooing and flossing and scraping food off pots, and to have those two variables combine in the April of one's life, if just for an hour, is worth venerating.

"You guys are fun," Claire said to me, and the plural subject and the rest of the sentence shot another little charge through me: Billy and I were not only *having* fun, we *were* fun, a tandem already making adventures together.

Naomi proposed we all go back to our apartment. We jumped into a cab, the three of them laughing in the backseat, the city sliding by in a heady blur. I kept turning my head to look at them through the pane of Plexiglas to catch whatever they were laughing at but could never quite hear the full exchange.

I bought two six-packs from the corner bodega and we drank in the living room, all of us talking buoyantly until Naomi asked Billy, "Which room is yours?"

"I'll show you," he said, and with no further discussion they left.

Claire and I smiled tightly at each other. The high of the dance floor had worn off and the presence of other people could no longer distract us. She flicked hair over her ears. I jiggled my cross-legged foot.

"I have something important to tell you," she said.

Several seconds ticked by.

"I'm trying to come up with a funny line, but I don't have anything," she said. "I'm awkward in these situations."

"Well," I said, "you want to see my room?"

She laughed. "Yeah, I'd love to see your etchings."

To avoid another uncomfortable silence I turned on the clock radio. Claire sat on the bed and surveyed the bookshelves in the dim light from a reading lamp.

"Do you ever go to a bookshop and look to see where your book would be on the shelf alphabetically? Like who you'd be next to?" she asked.

"Once or twice," I told her, though it was more often than that.

"I do it *every* time," she said. "How pathetically narcissistic is that? Especially because I tell myself I write so I can produce something for others. Like I'm doing the world some great service by providing access to my brain."

"I don't think it's that narcissistic. At least you're creating something new, not destroying anything."

"A lot of dead white men over here," she observed.

She was right; most of the authors on the jagged skyline of hardcover slabs and skinny paperbacks were white men and long gone. I didn't have much of a defense for the first two aspects of their identities, but death had always conferred mystique and genius for me; I doubt I would have mythologized them so much had they been contemporaries.

"I guess I aspire to join their ranks someday," I said.

"I can guarantee you'll be a dead white man someday."

"I mean more that I've always thought I'd be satisfied if I could write something that outlived me," I said. "Just one book, even. I wouldn't even mind if it were published posthumously, if it meant someone would pick it up in a hundred years."

"Jesus!" she said. "I just want to write a book a few people might like now, but you want your name to live on *forever*. Such a typical male." She gently elbowed me in the ribs. "Look on my works, ye mighty, and despair."

"Most people want to leave behind something of themselves," I said. "A book's a pretty modest way of doing it."

"You're right — chops down a few trees but doesn't cause overpopulation." She thumbed through *Winesburg, Ohio* and read aloud the title of the first chapter: " 'The Book of the Grotesque.' "

"Have you read that?" I asked.

"Nope. Any good?"

"That book made me want to be a writer the first time I read it."

"When was that?"

"Thirteen."

"So you decided to become a writer *just* when puberty was striking," she said. "What an incredible coincidence — so did I. I'm assuming the teenage years were as fun for you as they were for me."

Though I'd always thought that two writers dating each other would be disastrous (writers were either histrionic or reserved or oscillated wildly between the two poles, all we'd have to talk about would be what we'd composed that day or how we were depressed that we hadn't produced anything, the whole thing would be insular and incestuous), and the geography presented more than a few hurdles, I started fantasizing about a literary life with Claire, the clichés cribbed from Woody Allen movies, with us editing each other's work and attending readings and book parties together, and then doing all the normal things together that I had never done with anyone in my history of one-night stands and two-week flings (spending a long weekend in bed, traveling to a country neither of us had been to, assimilating into the other's family). It seemed so easy, all of a sudden, the way men of my parents' generation made it sound in the origin stories of their marriages: you met a girl when you were young, you hit it off, you ended up together. That I'd so seldom entertained these romantic flights of fancy with new partners was itself an unhealthy sign of the carapace I'd constructed for myself over the years; you had to allow your heart to open enough for it to be hurt, and mine was clamped shut like the shell of a stubborn pistachio, with just a sliver of space for only the most motivated prier.

The opening piano salvo of Bob Seger's "We've Got Tonight" thumped away on the radio. "I love this song," Claire said. She sang the first two lines, and then, perhaps realizing the embarrassing concordance of our situation and the next couplet, belted it out in a jauntily operatic voice: *Still here we are, both of us lonely, longing for shelter, from all that we see."*

Until that point, I'd assumed that nearly everyone bore a certain amount of loneliness within them, it was just the human condition of being trapped inside one mind and body for a lifetime, so that whatever isolation I felt was normal and universal; but hearing Seger's lyrics, rather than identifying with someone else's expression of similar feelings, as art was supposed to do for its audience, I thought that there was a different quality to mine, it was singular and peculiar and grotesque, a lonely flavor of loneliness — but maybe, I also reasoned, that's what true loneliness was, its Tolstoyan uniqueness made it so, and the only way out was to define yours to someone else and hope they still accepted you, and the only lonelier fate than rejection was never exposing yourself to its possibility.

I kissed her. After I turned off the reading lamp, we shed our clothes and slid under the sheet. When it seemed like the inevitable next step, I fumbled inside the drawer of my nightstand.

"What's that?" Claire asked.

"Condom," I said, pulling one out. "That all right?"

"Absolutely not. I was hoping to get an

95

STD from a guy I just met." She laughed before turning sober. "You *are* clean, aren't you?"

"I am."

"So we can do without it, then, and I'll just carry your love child back to England," she said. "Joking. Use it."

But as I unwrapped the package, I felt my arousal rapidly dwindling. I tried mentally reviving my erection to no avail.

"What's wrong?" she asked.

"I . . . sort of lost it there," I admitted.

"Oh," she said. "That's okay. Here, let me help."

Her hand traveled down my stomach to fondle me. It felt good, but I was too nervous to enjoy it and remained flaccid. Then the other hand reached farther down.

"Huh," she said with an awkward, confused giggle as she groped around.

"Don't," I said, pushing both her hands away. "Don't worry about it. I just drank too much."

She retracted her arms and lay on her back. I grabbed the boxers I'd placed on my nightstand and, without getting out of bed, wriggled into them. Neither of us spoke for a minute.

"I'm really tired," I said. "That's also part of it. I shouldn't have had that last beer."

"That's all right." Her voice was warm, reassuring. "It's like rain on your wedding day."

"Just bad luck," I said.

We were quiet again.

"Okay if we go to sleep?" I asked.

"Of course," she said.

I turned away from her. Our breathing and the wheezing of a garbage truck were the only sounds. After some time — five minutes? an hour? — her hand grazed the center of my back, testing if I was awake; the tentative gesture of someone in a foreign stranger's room, in the middle of the night, right then and there in an apartment, at an inflection point that could conceivably determine whether two people might some-day get married or never see each other again, both of us lonely and longing for shelter.

I pretended to be asleep.

The next morning we all went to breakfast at a cheap Polish diner on Twelfth and First, passing the naïve optimists lined up outside a trendier place down the block.

"In Soviet Russia, people wait on bread line," Billy said, imitating Yakov Smirnoff. "In America, people wait on brunch line. What a country!"

The nerves that had rattled him the night before had vanished; he and Naomi were cozily affectionate, his arm draped around her shoulders in the booth, her hand twirling his forelocks. I marveled at his comfort level just fourteen hours after he'd been a dumbstruck teenager in her presence.

And sex had been the catalyst for their intimacy, whereas the aloofness that had wedged itself between Claire and me after my failure had calcified overnight.

"Do you have a lot of reading for school?" she asked politely through bites of her blintz.

"We take three classes plus workshop."

"That's a lot."

"Yeah."

I felt guilty about my mumbly responses, felt bad for her that she'd been saddled with me and not Billy. My hangover provided something of an excuse, but I wanted to wipe the whole evening from memory as soon as possible.

Claire and Naomi had to get to the airport after breakfast, so we hailed a cab for them to retrieve their bags at their hotel. Billy and Naomi kissed in front of us and promised to write.

"Well, thanks for showing us around," Claire said to me.

"No problem." After a mutual stutter with our arms, we hugged.

"So, you liked her?" Billy asked me when their cab took off.

"Yeah. You?"

He nodded and knocked his pack of cigarettes against the butt of his palm. "She's very outwardly confident, but she's different in private."

"Most people are," I said.

"Thank God she had condoms, or I was about to knock on your door and ask you for one." He smiled. "Or *three*. Nah, just one. How was it for you?"

"Good," I said. "You want to head back home?"

"I was thinking of going to church."

"Yeah, me too."

"I'm serious, actually," he said. "I try to go once in a while."

"Shit," I said. "Sorry for laughing. I don't know anyone who — I thought you were joking."

"You want to come? I don't believe in God or anything," he said. "It's just a nice place to sit with your thoughts."

"That's okay," I said. "I'll see you at home."

We parted ways, and I went back to the apartment and read from a Richard Yates collection. I tried not to think about Claire — successfully, for the most part. Billy returned later and worked in his room. I nodded off on my bed in the afternoon, and when I awoke it was dark. I stumbled out to the living room couch and flipped through our seven TV stations. Everything on was football or something equally boring to me except for channel 11, which was playing the opening to *Field of Dreams.* I'd never seen it before, just parts, but out of groggy inertia I watched the first sequence, a greatest-hits voice-over biography of Kevin Costner's long-dead and semi-estranged fictional father.

"*Field of Dreams,*" I informed Billy as he came into the living room in a similar fog. "I've never seen it all the way through before."

"Me neither, somehow," he said. "It looked cheesy."

"We must be the only two guys in America," I said and made room on the couch. At a commercial break we ordered pizza and opened beers. The movie was entertaining, if saccharine. At the end, Costner reunites with his father, reincarnated as a young, ethereally handsome catcher. Without acknowledging their relationship, the two men discuss whether his homemade baseball field is heaven or Iowa and have a prolonged goodbye handshake before concluding with one final, loaded pump. His father walks away to the cornfields, and Costner's mouth opens and closes, as if he's trying to say something but can't articulate it, or is afraid to.

"Hey, Dad?" he manages with boyish vulnerability. "You want to have a catch?"

I'd been steeling myself against the movie's mawkishness, but I was only so strong. I turned my head away from Billy as the two men had a catch under the Iowan sunset. When the credits rolled, Billy went to the bathroom. I dried my eyes on my sleeve, collected the beer bottles in a plastic bag, and, to give myself time to recover, dropped them down the garbage chute in the hallway, where I waited, as I always did, for the muffled shattering to echo up to me — a sound that brought a childish thrill.

Billy was flattening and folding the pizza box when I came back. In the lamplight his eyes looked glassy, too.

I cleared my throat. "Well," I said in a hokey voice, "I sure do hope to have a catch like that with my own boy in a cornfield someday."

He laughed. Then he looked serious.

"You know, as corny — no pun intended

— as it sounds, that does sound kind of nice," he said.

"I thought you didn't want to have kids," I said.

"What makes you say that?"

"You said your ex-girlfriend wanted to have them and you didn't."

"Yeah — not right away, but someday. You don't?"

"I haven't really thought about it much," I said. "I guess I worry it'd get in the way of my writing. Like that guy from last night."

"There's that," he acknowledged. "But I always thought it would be sort of an empty life. Not just from not having kids around, but just not procreating, period."

"What do you mean?"

"Like it's an unnatural thing for a member of the species to do," he said. "Especially for a man. That's basically our reason for being, you know? Spread our seed. I'd be sort of sad if that was it for me, end of the line."

"Well, there are other ways to make a mark," I said, but he either ignored this or didn't hear me as he took the box and our greasy plates into the kitchen.

"Hey, thanks again, man," he said from inside. "You really saved me with this apartment. I'm pretty sure I would've left after the semester if not for you."

"You're welcome," I said. "That was a fun weekend."

4

Neither of us had classes on Mondays. That morning I lurched into the kitchen to find Billy rooting around under the sink, a pair of old rubber gloves and a roll of paper towels already out on the floor.

"You don't have to do this," I told him.

"It's cool," he said.

I'd consented to his condition of cleaning the apartment only so that he'd accept my help, and now that he was determined to go through with it, I really didn't want him to. "Seriously, don't," I said. "Or at least I should do it with you."

"This is what we agreed on." He pulled out a bottle of cleaning spray that was itself filthy. "It's how I earn my keep."

He refused to allow me to assist him. The job ahead was daunting; I hauled out my great-aunt's old vacuum cleaner only a couple of times a year and ignored vast swaths of the apartment. I said he didn't have to touch my room, to which I retreated after breakfast so I wouldn't have to be near him while he started in the kitchen. Later I heard him vacuuming through my closed door. When he switched to the bathroom, I couldn't bear sitting idle in the apartment and yelled that I was running out for some errands.

I dithered around the neighborhood for an hour, trawling the fluorescent aisles of Gristedes for things I didn't really need under oppressive soft rock; a strong peacetime economy under a moderate government yields terrible mainstream art. When I came back, the apartment had molted its soiled skin. Billy had wiped off years of First Avenue debris from the windowsills. The double-basin sink looked like beautiful ivory canyons. Most incredibly, the grout in the shower was nearly white; the frayed toothbrush he'd used on the showerhead rested on the side of the tub, proof of his elbow grease. I knew my apartment had been dirty and that my perfunctory swipes with paper towels had kept it barely habitable, but the deep clean jolted me. I'd become acclimated to living in squalor for years and never thought it was anything beyond standard bachelor dirtiness.

I knocked on his bedroom door. He was

reading Kafka's *The Trial.* "It's like a brand-new apartment," I told him.

"It shouldn't take as long in the future, now that there's a clean base," he said.

I still felt uneasy about it and at lunchtime asked if he wanted me to pick him up anything at the Chinese restaurant on Sixteenth and First that I ordered from two or three times a week; I planned to turn down his money after. He was sitting on his bed, writing in a large notebook.

"No thanks," he said. "I'm gonna run to the supermarket."

I called in my order and walked down to get it. "Hello!" said the older woman behind the counter. She was the closest I'd come to any degree of neighborly familiarity, though she gave the same effusive greeting to all customers, so I could never tell if she recognized me or not. When I returned, Billy was unpacking two Gristedes shopping bags. Among other things, he'd bought two jars of mustard.

"I have mustard," I said.

"I use a lot of it," he said.

I ate my General Tso's chicken at my desk while trying to read the short story in that week's *New Yorker,* the entirety of which took place inside the head of an uninvited guest at a dinner party. Soon I heard Billy typing at his computer. I arched my back and leaned over. He was in profile, hunched over his notebook in his lap like a monk studying a manuscript, hunting and pecking at the keyboard with one hand while he ate a sandwich from the other.

He came to me later that afternoon with a 3.5-inch floppy disk in hand. "Could I use your printer and pay you back for the ink and paper?" he asked.

"Of course, and you don't have to pay me back," I said.

I relinquished my chair, and he slid his disk into my computer. "It's just five pages," he said as my dot matrix screeched out the lines. "I'll buy more paper."

"You want to trade?" I asked. "I'm working on a story and could use fresh eyes."

"Sure thing," he said.

I had abandoned *The Copy Chief,* figuring it would be more efficient to fail better at short stories, and was halfway through an Orwellian, allegorical one, about a hippie summer camp whose director grows mad with power and turns it into a dictatorial communist work camp. In the unwritten second half, a rebellious counselor would lead an insurrection against him, exiling the director to a nearby island without a canoe and winning over the fetching Nadia, with the ominous suggestion that he, too, will be corrupted by power.

We exchanged printouts. Billy took "Camp Redwood" into his room, and I read the second chapter of *No Man's Land*. Though I would have liked to be able to point to a real flaw and prove my usefulness, I had nothing to add aside from correcting a few erroneous commas and the like.

"I wouldn't change anything," I said when he was ready to talk. "I just fixed a couple of style things. The way you used 'however,' you have to put a semicolon or period before, not a comma."

"Thanks, man," he said.

"And you've got some reps that I circled."

"Reps?"

"Word repetitions. Copyediting term."

He nodded and handed me my story. As with *The Copy Chief,* it was a tangle of red-inked curlicues and cross-outs and rejiggered sentences.

"You're great with plot," he said. "The main thing I was looking for was more between Paul and Nadia."

I reviewed his notes when he left. In one of the scenes with Nadia, he'd written in the margins, "What does Nadia do for Paul, other than be beautiful? What's he missing that she supplies? What's his 'invisible damage'? (Ha.)"

I applied all his line edits to the prose and did my best to respond to his questions about Nadia and Paul, coming up with a backstory about Paul's parents divorcing that closely resembled my own. At dinnertime, Billy knocked on my door.

"Want anything special for dinner?" he asked.

"You really don't have to cook for me," I said. "I can get takeout."

"I'm already cooking for myself, so it's not a big deal to make a little more. And I'm not a gourmet chef, just to warn you. How about pasta with chicken and vegetables?"

I told him that sounded good. By the time I reemerged from my room, he'd cooked the whole meal, which we ate at the four-seat dining table. It was tasty but needed seasoning, and I found a block of Parmesan in the fridge from a high-end store on Third Avenue. "Want some?" I asked after I grated it.

"Thanks," he said. "And this is awkward, but do you mind chipping in for the groceries?"

"Shit, can't believe I forgot." I dug a ten-dollar bill out my pocket. "This enough?"

"That's way more than half."

"Keep it," I said, pushing it across the table. "You did all the cooking."

I sensed our economic arrangement was going to surface frequently in conversation from his side. I didn't want him to feel indebted to me or like a freeloader, but there really was no good way to discuss it.

"Wonder what's going to happen in O.J.'s civil trial," I said to change the subject.

This more or less became our routine that fall. We read and wrote a lot at home, we edited each other's work (I remained the disproportionate beneficiary, though he seemed grateful for my mechanical corrections). Billy made all his lunches — usually tuna or sardine sandwiches with extravagant lubrications of mustard — and prepared us simple, hearty dinners a few times a week. He cleaned the entire apartment, save for my room, on Sunday afternoons, sometimes after going to church, which he never invited me to again and which I didn't ask about. I consistently made up an excuse to be out while he did it. I didn't mind lounging while he cooked, but I felt too uncomfortable sitting at my desk while he was on his knees at the tub, scrubbing away my dead skin cells.

I saw NYU friends less and less, the distance from our school days reminding me that we hadn't been all that close in the first place.

Billy had never been much of a television watcher, but when our week of classes had concluded on Thursdays, I got him into NBC's "Must See TV" lineup. Sitting on the couch with him in front of the glowing electronic hearth as nearly forty million Americans also watched *Seinfeld* and *Friends* at the exact same time became a comforting ritual, especially since, in the past, I had tended to grow a little depressed after plowing through that two-hour block alone. (I stopped before *ER,* never having liked medical dramas.)

After workshop, we'd play darts with our classmates before we both repaired to the Eagle's Nest. I often swung by on his other nights there, occasionally staying until his shift was over. The MFA students started throwing parties at their Morningside Heights apartments or arranging nights out at bars. We always went together and mostly stayed by each other's side.

"I can't think of a single fucking thing to say to these people," he told me at one party that October, in reference to our classmates.

"The weather is an evergreen topic," I

said. "In the summer, I recommend saying, 'It's not the heat, it's the humidity,' and when it gets cold, people are impressed when you complain about the wind chill."

He rarely laughed at these kinds of jokes but smiled just enough to make me feel my effort had not been in vain. "But maybe I never really knew how to talk to anyone, and I just anesthetized myself with beer so I wouldn't notice."

"Join the club," I said.

"But you're not a joiner."

"Neither are you."

"So that makes this," he said, "our own little club of two."

He did, however, know how to talk to women, or at least knew that he didn't need to do much to attract their attention. Either his time in New York or the experience with Naomi had unburdened him of his Midwestern inferiority complex, and he began sleeping with female grad students and women he met at bars. He went to their place every time, out of respect, I assumed, for me.

"You know, you can bring women back here," I said to him once when he showed up at the apartment on a Sunday afternoon, hair mussed and happily hung over. "I don't mind."

"All right," he said, but he never did it.

I'd long been curious how, exactly, other people who had their days mostly to themselves filled them up. I wasn't so much a procrastinator as a time waster, getting my work done and then frittering away the spare hours with lackadaisical urgency, half-reading a handful of magazine articles and roaming stores for thirty minutes when five would suffice. Billy was ruthlessly economical with his limited freedom. No matter how late he'd been out or how much he'd drunk the previous night, he wrote at least a little the next day, and when he didn't have the handicaps of a hangover or external commitments, he was a pack mule, working hours without a break. I derived real pleasure from having made it easier for him, through both financial relief and giving him something of a room of his own. When I heard him tapping away at his desk, I felt the kind of satisfaction I felt when setting a kettle on a lit stove while washing dishes, knowing that another task was being simultaneously completed without my assistance but that I was ultimately responsible for it.

"Where's your other half?" a girl from the program asked me at that party in October, when he was in the bathroom.

"What do you mean?"

"Billy. You guys are, like, attached at the hip."

For some reason I laughed. "We're just roommates," I said.

Billy and I sat together in Dodge Hall for one of the weekly readings at school, by a decorated poet on the upswing of an academic career: an associate professor certain to receive tenure somewhere, not yet beset by the injuries of time and disappointment and irrelevance, future promise still outweighing his track record. After a second-year student introduced him for ten minutes, reciting block quotes only to uncork a three-word exegesis, he advanced to the lectern in an elaborately knotted scarf and stood there silently for perhaps twenty seconds before launching, without preamble, into full-bore "poet voice," that unnatural cadence and breathy tone used at readings and nowhere else in the world. I was typically unable to track poems read aloud, but this one was so facile that it was hard not to — and yet each Hallmark sentiment and cheap irony elicited murmurs and demonstrative, knowing *hmm*s from audience members.

He finished the poem and, in a perfectly normal and pleasant speaking voice, explicated what he had just read, its inspiration, the struggles he'd had during the writing process, his well-known poet friends who had helped him "figure it out through endless revisions and pots of black coffee," as if what they'd all collaborated on had the magnitude of the Manhattan Project — even though, he coquettishly admitted, "I'm still not sure what it all means." He read more poems and during the interludes was a fount of bromides, exhorting us to "let yourself bleed on the page" so we could "write something true" with an awestruck reverence suggesting it was an original sentiment.

"What we do is important," he said to nods of agreement, and then, as if we hadn't been able to understand him the first time, repeated himself twice as loudly, with syllabic emphasis: "What we *do* is *im-por-tant.*"

Billy snickered quietly.

The poet thumbed through his Post-it-flagged book. "Okay, I'll just read . . ." he said, and I was buoyed by the prospect of imminent liberation, I wanted to be anywhere else with the impassioned urgency that few things outside of a tedious literary reading can instigate, until he delivered the devastating verdict: "three more poems." The first two were blessedly short, but for his final long poem, after each stanza, he silently snapped his fingers while mouthing "One, two, three, four," to keep some sort of metrical beat.

With his hand below his knee, Billy stealthily mimicked the soundless snapping in sync with the poet.

"Stop," I whispered, but Billy kept doing it. "Stop."

"Stop," he mimicked me, which made me want to laugh harder. We were inconsiderate fifth graders unable to behave ourselves, but we both found it funnier and funnier, until he no longer needed to imitate the poet's action; the suppression of our laughter became the very source of our amusement. I hadn't had that experience since high school and had forgotten how scarily pleasurable it was, the defiance and simultaneous fear of authority shared with a peer.

At last the poet stopped reading.

"It's funny how the poems I'm most proud of are about the things I'm most ashamed of," he said.

I waited for Billy to scoff again; never had I seen such a shameless exhibitionist, and his last poem had addressed a second-person lover to whom the speaker was regrettably incapable of committing, hardly the stuff of bone-deep mortification.

116

But Billy discreetly took out his notepad and wrote down the sentence.

David Lankford, a college friend who had recently started as an editorial assistant at a publishing house, said he could get me on the guest list of a party the literary magazine *Open City* was throwing. I was excited — I hadn't been to any publishing-industry gatherings aside from a stodgy book party at the National Arts Club for an older family friend — and asked if he could put Billy's name down, too.

"Sure," Billy said when I invited him.

When I knocked on his door the night of the party, he was sewing a button onto a long-sleeved shirt. A kit with a pink floral design was on the bed. It had to have been my great-aunt's, though I'd never seen it around the apartment before.

"Where'd you find the sewing kit?" I asked.

"It's mine," he said.

"Right, your dad gave it to you when you turned fourteen," I joked. "Where was it, the back of the linen closet?"

He tested the give of the button. "No, it's really mine. I don't remember when I got it."

"Oh," I said. "There's a tailor down the

block, if you ever need it."

He shrugged and snipped the remaining thread with a small pair of scissors.

The event was held on a Thursday night at a SoHo loft accessed by a freight elevator with a manually operated grate. It opened up to a foyer with a huge photograph on the wall of a nude man, his toned, coiled body shrouded in chiaroscuro but his penis dangling in outline. Billy glanced at it for a few seconds.

Beyond that was a roomful of trim people who were young or aggressively fending off middle age, the women almost all in black, the men in the publishing uniform of open-necked shirts and blazers, chinos denoting industry professionals and jeans for the writers, nearly everyone gesticulating with a cigarette or sloshing drink. A Yorkie scurried about, yapping at boot heels and square-toed oxfords and jumping onto the bright angular furniture. Nonsense lyrics from a Pavement song tumbled out of recessed speakers.

A woman with a clipboard guarded the foyer and asked for our names. "And we're also requesting donations for our friend Samantha's gender reassignment surgery," she said, pointing to a metal box stuffed with cash. I dropped in a five-dollar bill. Billy

118

slowly parted with two singles.

I didn't see David when we entered the fray, so we positioned ourselves by the food and alcohol, glugging red wine and eating endives dolloped with sour cream and iridescent beads of roe. Billy fed his first one warily into his mouth, as though it might bite him. A few famous people, or at least downtown–New York famous, were in attendance, stirring up a frisson among the upscale civilians spying in the same direction while pretending indifference.

A man and a woman near us erupted into paroxysms of delight upon greeting each other. They air-kissed and talked about the last time they'd been in the same place, "ages ago at George's," before sliding into shop talk about a young writer the woman was editing whose debut novel was going to be excerpted in an upcoming *New Yorker* and had "sold in sixteen territories."

"You see your friend? Or anyone you know?" Billy asked, tapping his LA Gear–shod foot.

"No. Except for the people who are famous."

"Yeah? Who're they?"

"Well, that's Mary Gaitskill," I said, nodding subtly in her direction. "The woman by the window wrote *Prozac Nation,* Eliza-beth Wurtzel. That's the actress Parker Posey by that pillar, and I'm pretty sure the guy she's talking to is Noah Baumbach, who directed her in *Kicking and Screaming.*"

"Never heard of any of them," Billy said.

We kept watching. Two men not much older than us, both in turtlenecks, walked by, heads thrown back in hysterics.

"These people look like poseurs," Billy said.

"Some of them," I allowed.

He drained his wineglass and refilled it close to the brim. "At least Samantha will finally be reassigned to her correct gender. Or his. I couldn't tell if that was the new name or the old name."

"It's probably the new one," I said. "So 'her.' "

He smirked.

"What?"

"C'mon," he said. "Gender reassignment surgery?"

"What about it?"

"Forget it." It looked like he was indeed going to drop it, but after a moment he continued. "People can do what they want to their own bodies. But if you want to get surgery for something optional like that, pay for that shit yourself. It isn't cancer. And everyone here" — he twirled his hand —

"probably ignored a dozen bums begging for change on their way to the party, but they're happy to give a handout for this."

"That's probably true," I said. I thought about pressing him on his skepticism, but trotting out the terms I'd learned in numerous seminars at NYU — social constructs, gender performativity, spectrums and continuums — wasn't going to disarm his prejudices. I doubted he had encountered these ideas, let alone real-life examples, much in Illinois, if at all. He probably didn't even know any openly gay people. A year or two in New York would be more persuasive than any argument I could come up with.

We were granted a reprieve as David, in wire-rimmed glasses and a tailored suit, hugged me hello and introduced himself to Billy. "So you're also taking workshop with Sylvia Hellman?" David asked Billy. "I absolutely love her work."

"She's a good teacher," Billy said with a stiff nod.

David proprietarily squeezed my shoulder. "And how's this gentleman's writing? Should I be preempting his book now before he stirs up a hideously obscene bidding war?"

David had always been ostentatious, especially at parties, and I'd never cared before, but for the first time I became embarrassed by his affectations.

"He's a talented writer," said Billy.

"Did you see Ethan Hawke here before?" David said under his breath. "I'd *kill* to be publishing his novel."

"It's good?" I asked.

"I haven't read it yet," he said, unapologetically craning his head over me at, surely, someone more important. "I should mingle. There are a bunch of up-and-coming young agents here, if you want an introduction later."

"That'd be great," I said.

After he left, Billy asked, "How long have you known him, again?"

"Just since the end of college," I said. "I was friends with his girlfriend first. I'm not really that close with him."

"*That guy* has a girlfriend?"

"Not right now, I don't think. In college he did."

Billy finished his glass of wine. "I think I'm gonna get out of here."

"It'll get better," I told him.

"No offense" — he took another look at the room — "but this isn't my scene. I don't want to spend my time kissing agents' asses."

"Fair enough," I said, though I was disappointed to miss out on David's connections; Sylvia would probably send Billy to her agent, but I needed all the help I could get. "Want to go somewhere else?"

We found a down-at-heel bar on the corner. Within five minutes a woman with a nose ring and a leather jacket struck up a conversation with Billy. Soon they were sitting side by side, knees knocking under the bar, as if they'd known each other for years yet still had the charged attraction of strangers. Watching her fall under his spell, I wondered if Billy understood how handsome he was and if that was the innate source of his confidence around women, or if he wasn't fully aware of it, as he seemed not to be about his writing talent. He wasn't vain; he certainly put no effort into his clothing, and I never once saw him fuss with his hair or preen in a mirror. Maybe that was it: he didn't even consider his appearance, because it had never caused any problems for him. There was not thinking about something because you wanted to ignore it, and not thinking about it because you were utterly unselfconscious.

One of the woman's friends showed up, but it became clear within seconds that she didn't want anything to do with me. Billy nevertheless curled his arm around my back like an impresario touting his performer. "This guy right here's the next F. Scott Fitzgerald," he said. "He's going to stir up an obscene bidding war for his book."

He'd done a similar routine before at parties. While I appreciated his good-faith attempts to get me involved — our success rates in this department were as asymmetric as possible, discounting his first night in the apartment — it was emasculating, as if I didn't have the wherewithal to navigate the world of women on my own.

"No, stay, man," he said when I told him I was going home. "We're about to do shots. It won't be fun without you."

"Nah, I'm tired," I said. I walked out, but a stout man, with razor burn all over his neck that nearly matched his reddish crew cut, blocked me near the door. "Lemme get a cigarette?" he said. He sounded drunk and appeared to be by himself.

I took out my pack, but it was empty. "All out, sorry."

"Yo, lemme get a cigarette," he repeated.

"I don't have any," I said, showing him the carton.

He pushed me. It wasn't forceful, but I was unprepared and staggered back. The people around us either didn't notice or care. My fight-or-flight response spiked, all the latter. I'd never been in an altercation in my life, let alone a bar fight.

"Fuckin' pussy," he said. "Give me a fuckin' cigarette."

Before I could react, I felt a hand on my shoulder, and Billy's body moved in front of mine. "Here, man," he said, holding out a cigarette. The guy eyed it warily, as if the peace offering were a trap — Billy was stronger, bigger, younger — before taking it and retreating to a barstool.

"Fucking guy," Billy said as he escorted me to the door. "You did the right thing, not escalating it. You good?"

"Yeah, thanks," I said, feeling both grateful to him and ashamed that I'd needed him to rescue me; we both knew that escalation wasn't in my physical vocabulary. The subway was right there, but I took a cab home.

The next morning I was awoken by the phone ringing.

"It's me," Billy whispered when I answered. "Sorry if I woke you. I'm at this girl's place, and I don't know how to get home."

"Why don't you ask her?"

"She's still asleep. And to be honest, I didn't" — he chuckled — "I didn't perform that well last night. It was bad. I just want

125

to get out of here."

"Happens to the best of us," I said. "What neighborhood are you in?"

"No idea. We took a cab here and went over a bridge, that's all I remember. And I have almost no money."

"So you're not in Manhattan. Can you see a street sign out the window?"

"No," he said. "It's almost like the suburbs. Lots of trees."

"You're probably in Brooklyn, maybe Queens," I said. "Look for a piece of mail addressed to her. I've got a map of New York City with a street index, and I can tell you which subway to take."

He left and returned in a minute. "It says Daniel Low Terrace."

I located the street in the index and cross-referenced it with the map.

"Shit," I said. "You're in Staten Island. Or on it."

"Fuck me. How do I get home?"

Like most New Yorkers, I'd never been and wasn't sure. "Take a cab. I'm sure there's an ATM nearby."

"I don't take my ATM card with me when I go out," he said.

"Ring up when you get here and I'll spot you."

"How much would it be, you think?"

"I'm guessing a lot," I said. "Or you know what? You're pretty close to the Staten Island ferry. Ask someone for directions, take that, and then the subway home. I think the ferry's fifty cents. Do you have that on you?"

"Yeah. But not enough for the subway, too."

"Take a cab after the ferry. I'll cover you when you get here. It won't be too expensive."

"Thanks, man," he said.

I went back to sleep, and when I woke up again a few hours later, Billy still wasn't home. As I read the *Times* and waited for my French press to brew at the dining table, he opened the door, sweaty and disheveled.

"I didn't hear you ring up," I said. "Is the cab still downstairs?"

"I walked from the ferry." He pointed to the French press. "Can I have some of that?"

I poured it for him. He took a sip and closed his eyes.

"Oh, Jesus." He opened his eyes, clapped a hand on my collarbone, and released an exhausted breath. "I am so fucking happy to see you."

"Welcome home, sailor," I said.

I was walking to the Eagle's Nest the next

Saturday night when I noticed the Russian and Turkish Baths were just a few storefronts away. People at NYU had spoken highly of them, but I'd never been despite living ten blocks away. I was about to go into the bar when I realized that it would be unlike anything Billy had been to in Illinois, a novel New York experience disconnected from money and status, the opposite of a poseur-filled publishing party.

I bought two eighteen-dollar admissions for Sunday, the only available day in the near future; the two owners were in a longtime quarrel, apparently, alternating weeks on duty, and neither would honor passes purchased from the other. At the Eagle's Nest, I asked Billy if he wanted to go.

"How much does it cost?"

"I have two gift cards that I have to use by tomorrow," I said.

The next afternoon we made our way to the building. A sign outside read THE STRAIGHT PLACE.

"Does that mean what I think it means?" Billy asked. "In terms of what bathhouses are known for?"

"I think so," I said. "A little Eastern European homophobia."

Sunday turned out to be a men-only day.

In the locker room I stripped down to the bathing suit that I'd worn under my jeans, but Billy, his back to me, completely disrobed and wrapped a towel around his waist. I turned away until he was ready, and we padded out to the Russian Room, heated with a rock-warmed oven. A passel of hirsute Russian men reposed on the benches, nude and chatting in their mother tongue. Billy kept his towel on as we sat on the lowest bench, the least stifling level. It hurt when I inhaled, but the heat felt purifying, and I savored the rare time and place in which profuse sweating was fully sanctioned.

I'd seen his bare torso as he went into and out of the shower in Stuy Town, but not up close. He had a broad chest with a black knot of hair at the sternum and would have looked at home standing over the sink in a shaving cream commercial, marveling over the smoothness of his cheeks. I'd watched part of *The Silence of the Lambs* while channel surfing earlier that week, and Buffalo Bill's attempts to create a bodysuit of female skin inspired a brief, less gruesome mental scenario in which I somehow wore Billy's body like an exoskeleton, moving through the world in his impervious chassis.

We spoke little, conserving our energy, until I suggested we switch to the steam room, where we sat a foot apart. He reclined against the wall and sighed. The steam pumped out with new vigor, choking the room in a uniform fog.

"This was a good idea," he said. As another cloud of steam came out, he flapped his towel open to cool down. It had been tied on the side closer to me, and I saw an indistinct blur of his flesh. I looked ahead at the tiled wall.

"You ever hear from Naomi again?" I asked.

"Nope," he said. "You in touch with Claire?"

"No." I inhaled deeply, allowing the steam to gather and sit in my lungs. "I wouldn't mind seeing her again, though. We had fun."

The following week I received my second and final workshop for the semester, for "Camp Redwood." I went in with guarded optimism; it couldn't be worse than the last time.

"This feels overly programmatic," Sylvia said after some faint praise for the story's concept, "and written more out of an idea than anything else."

Everyone else agreed — other than Billy,

who was once again my sole defender. Their remarks were more courteously delivered this go-round, perhaps in recompense for the lashing from *The Copy Chief,* but it was another discouraging showing for me.

"Fuck 'em," Billy told me later at the Eagle's Nest. "These morons think good writing has to be filled with lists of flowers and shit." (One of the other stories discussed that week had contained a page-long paragraph with nothing but a paratactic catalog of the landscape's flora.)

"They're probably right about mine," I said, fishing for a compliment but also believing it.

"Want me to take another look at it tomorrow?" Billy asked.

I told him that I planned to forget about it and move on. But the next day he asked for his line-edited copy back, insisting that a few small changes might make a big difference. After a while with it in his room, he returned to mine.

"Can I edit this on the computer?" he asked. "It'll be easier, and then you can decide what edits you want to keep."

"You're wasting your time."

"Just let me take a crack at it," he said.

I saved it to a disk, and he went to work on his machine, typing all afternoon. By the time *Friends* started, he still wasn't finished.

"I appreciate it, but this is unsalvageable," I told him.

"Nothing's unsalvageable," he said with surprising conviction.

I didn't argue any further. Finally, just before he left for the Eagle's Nest on Friday, he handed back the disk. I read while he was gone. The story I'd workshopped was nearly unrecognizable. He'd preserved the setting, general narrative arc, and characters' names but rewritten the entire thing from scratch; hardly a sentence was undisturbed. Solely through the power of his prose, he was, once again, able to pull off the kind of termite-art approach I wished I had in my repertoire.

It was strange to recognize how much better he was and not sink into my customary feelings of envy or inadequacy but instead be flattered that of all the students in our program, I was the one he was choosing to help.

I popped down to the Eagle's Nest to thank him. The man in the tweed cap was at his usual post.

"It's so much better," I told Billy. "But it should have your name on it now, not mine."

"You laid the groundwork," he said. "I just

132

fine-tuned the language a little."

It was obvious he was downplaying his contribution, but I tried to accept his statement. Maybe this was just what a good editor did. Or a good friend.

"Well, thank you," I said. "No one's ever given this much attention to something of mine."

"It was fun to edit," he said. "You're John Stockton, I'm Karl Malone."

My confusion must have shown on my face.

"The Jazz players?" he said.

"I'm not really into jazz," I said.

He laughed. "The *Utah* Jazz. In the NBA."

I forced my own laugh.

The next week, without telling Billy or anyone else, I made twenty copies of the story at the neighborhood print shop to mail off to as many places, from the *New Yorker* and *Harper's* and the *Paris Review* on down to some small university journals listed in *Poets & Writers.*

After I dropped the envelopes off at the post office, I thought about how I could repay Billy. He didn't need my editing and was uninterested in the legwork of pursuing publication himself, but maybe he could still benefit from my network. When he was on campus one afternoon, I found, among all the archived copies of his edited workshop submissions and critiques in his file cabinet, clean versions of the first few chapters of *No Man's Land*. I xeroxed and mailed them to David Lankford, thinking optimistically of how it might someday change Billy's life.

"By my roommate (and the best writer in the MFA program at Columbia)," I wrote on a Post-it. "Maybe you'll preempt him before he starts a bidding war?"

After I picked up some Chinese food, a man entered my building behind me. As I held the door for him I noticed the Stuyvesant Town badge pinned to his blazer pocket. I crossed paths with someone from management once a month or so, and though it wasn't as if he could tell from looking at me that I lived there illegally, it always triggered a flutter in my heartbeat. He joined me in the elevator and reached out to press his floor button but stopped when he saw eight was already illuminated. When the door opened, he exited first and looked both ways before making a left.

"Don't go out for a little while," I whispered to Billy inside the apartment. "A guy from Stuy Town management's on the floor."

He nodded as his finicky computer

134

growled with indigestion from backing up his work to a disk, which he then placed inside his file cabinet. "That reminds me — I think you accidentally threw out a letter with some junk mail that looked like it had something to do with the apartment. I put it over there."

"It's the renewal for renter's insurance," I confirmed after opening the envelope. "My great-aunt keeps it going."

"What's the point, if she doesn't live here?"

"I guess to protect her furniture from fire or theft, in case she ever wants it back," I said. "She's on the neurotic side. I'll forward it."

"So now I don't have to worry about accidentally breaking her insane glass bottle collection," he joked.

Magic-hour rays of October sun were slanting into the living room, casting a reddish glow on his back, where the thin ribbed cotton of his white tank top hugged his body like a second skin. Aside from the computer, his outfit and the dingy walls produced an old-fashioned tableau of the writer at work in his oubliette. He even had an issue of *Time* from 1974 out on his desk, featuring Nixon's special prosecutor on the cover, that he'd found in the recesses of the entryway closet in a decaying magazine stack. All he needed was a dangling cigarette, a derby hat, and a tumbler of bourbon.

From my bedroom closet I retrieved my Polaroid camera, unused for a long time. "Let's take a picture of us writing," I said. "The light's good right now."

"Why?"

"Evidence," I said, "of our transient youth. We'll be nostalgic for it someday."

He looked apathetic. "I'll be too aware of you to write while you take the picture, so I'll just pretend to."

From a three-quarters angle behind him I pressed the button and waved the photo after the camera ejected it. Even in fuzzy resolution, the muscles in his shoulders were articulated, and a groove demarcated his deltoids from his triceps. I snapped another and asked him to take a couple of me at my desk. We divided up the photos so we got one of each. I ignored my picture and studied his. Despite his knowing I was taking a picture of him, despite his writing pose being just that, he appeared to be in deep concentration, concerned only with the screen in front of him — or not even with that, just his mind, the keyboard and monitor its mere input and output, a virtuoso musician's instruments. When I wrote, a speck on my monitor could distract me. My normal self-consciousness in photos was doubled in this one. I wasn't immersed in my thoughts; I was doing anything I could to get away from them.

Here was a real writer, his photos said, not only because of his single-mindedness, but because that focus suggested he was undaunted by the darkest corners of his psyche — that when he wrote, he wrote something true.

Billy had the night off for Halloween, and we went, sans costumes, to a Columbia party in Morningside Heights. The students who hosted it had the standard tight-squeeze railroad apartment for university housing. Seeing up close how my contemporaries lived — with multiple roommates, in a cheaply constructed building with windows that didn't seal out drafts and tacky linoleum — made me feel guilty, as always, for having Stuy Town at a fraction of the rent.

We stayed late, until about ten people were left. The conversation in the living room turned to the revealing Halloween costumes worn by women, which Henry, a fiction writer who had taped a piece of paper his shirt that read, in small Courier font, greetings, all hallows' eve revelers, i am al gore, maintained were "entirely of their own volition."

"No it's not," said a female poet dressed as Amelia Earhart. "They're conforming to cultural notions of what feminine sexuality is. They're reproducing sexual images of women that have been sanctioned largely by men."

"So you're saying they're mindless followers," Henry said.

"They're not mindless followers. They're being coerced by the dominant ideology."

"There are sexualized images of men in the culture. You don't see *them* showing off their bodies on Halloween. Except for maybe gay guys."

"It's completely different," she said. "And besides, what hypersexualized images of men — straight men — even exist? Other than that Diet Coke commercial with the construction worker?"

After deliberating, Henry answered, "The Red Hot Chili Peppers."

"Anthony Kiedis running with his shirt off in a video is *not* comparable to what I'm talking about."

"Not that," he said. "When they wear socks over their dicks."

A plume of smoke escaped through her

cackle. "I'll believe that the Red Hot Chili Peppers are a legitimate social force that influences young men when I see a bunch of guys wearing socks on their dicks at a Halloween party."

"Okay, then," Henry said. "I'll do it." After some back-and-forth in which the girl doubted his seriousness, he insisted he really would strip. It was unclear what the logic of agreeing to this was, other than as a prelude to getting the girls in attendance to remove their own items of clothing.

"You guys in?" he asked the other men in the room. Besides Billy and me, there were the two party hosts, one burly, one skinny, almost a caricature of an odd couple.

"Fuck it, why not," the burly one said.

"I've got tube socks in my room," said his roommate.

Billy and I shared a glance. I couldn't tell if he wanted to do it or not.

"Wait, wasn't this an episode of *Friends*?" a girl asked.

" 'The One Where They Put Socks on Their Penises,' " the burly host said as he headed down the hall.

"I think you're thinking of Ugly Naked Guy," said another girl.

"No, there's one when Chandler sees Rachel naked, so they make him show his dick to her to make up for it, but he won't do it," he said.

"They did it on *Seinfeld,* too," said the skinny host. "The shrinkage episode."

Henry, walking behind the two hosts, turned to Billy and me. "You coming?"

"I'm in," Billy said, following them. I brought up the rear.

In the bedroom, the burly host rummaged through his bureau and tossed pairs of socks to us. "How does this work? We stick our dicks through our boxers?" I asked.

"If you want to be a pussy," Henry said. "I'm going commando."

"Also *Seinfeld,*" the skinny host said. "Kramer freaks out about his sperm count and stops wearing underwear."

The other guys turned their backs. Costumes, jeans, and boxers fell to the floor in a jangle of belt buckles and keys and coins.

"Hold on," the burly host said. "How does the sock stay on the dick?"

"You have to wrap it over the balls, too. They keep it in place," said Henry.

"Ah, there's the rub," the guy said. "Literally. This feels sort of good. Nice and snug."

Everyone else was naked below the waist. I still hadn't unbuckled my belt. "Why, exactly, are we doing this?" I asked.

"Because we're young and drunk," said

the burly host.

"And it's *sexual,*" his roommate added. "And there are girls out there who will respond in kind to our brazen display of sexuality. Like a mating call."

There were some jokes made about peacocks as their hands fiddled at their midsections, making last-minute adjustments.

"You okay, man?" Billy asked me quietly.

"Yeah," I said. "It's just hot in here."

"Everyone almost ready?" Henry asked over his shoulder.

"It's late," I said. "I'm gonna go."

"Don't be Chandler, dude," he said.

"I'm not. I'm just tired."

"It'll cover up your peacock, if you're scared about looking inadequate."

Billy, half-naked, turned to look at me standing there, the only one fully clothed, two balled-up socks in my hand.

"I'm out, too," he said, pulling up his underwear and jeans. "This is lame. You're all getting naked together just to prove some political point? And you" — he pointed to the owner of the socks — "want to wear your socks after they've been all over our dicks?" He shook his head. "This is fucking gay, man."

No one answered him. "Let's get out of

here," he said and dropped his sock on the floor.

"Those guys suck," Billy said when we were out of the apartment. "Such sheep."

We took the subway home. "Should we hit up a bar?" he asked when we surfaced at Fourteenth. "I kind of want to hang out more."

I assumed his desire to extend the night was really about finding a woman to go home with, and I didn't feel like going to a bar just to hold his coat once again. "You can go," I said. "I don't have a bar in me."

"Then how about we drink outside for a little while?"

"What do you mean?"

"It's not that cold. Let's get some whiskey and find a bench."

"There's a liquor store down the block that's probably still open," I said, a little touched.

We bought a half pint of whiskey at the store and two Snapples at a bodega and took them to the courtyard behind our building, sitting on a bench by the concrete rectangle that scampering children and roller hockey players commandeered in the daytime. I'd smoked there by myself hundreds of times after hours. Other Stuy Town buildings surrounded us, lending it the feel of an open-air enclosure set off from the rest of the city. Billy chugged his Snapple — I dumped mine out — and we decanted the whiskey into the empty bottles.

"Nice clouds," Billy said of a herd that was scudding over the moon. "Like a tattered wedding dress."

We drank for a minute without talking, rinsed in a mild breeze that lifted the sweet rot of wet leaves.

"This setup feels like we should be exploring the big questions," he said. He was on to something; silent outdoor experiences like this, in an acre of space without a person in sight, were rare in New York City. There was a reason fictional male bonding stories, in which characters convey deep sentiments to each other without words, typically take place sequestered in nature.

"Please don't ask me what the meaning of life is," I said.

"Of course not. How about . . ." He took a contemplative drag of his cigarette. "What's your biggest fear?"

I wasn't sure if it was a joke. "I don't know," I said with a chuckle.

The tree branches around us rattled. Halloween revelers shouted in the distance. I got the feeling he wanted an earnest answer.

"Maybe that no one will ever really know

143

me," I said.

"That's a good one," he said.

"You?"

He stared straight ahead into the empty play area and swallowed a mouthful of whiskey, already nearly done with his. Nearly everyone our age drank to excess, but his appetite was truly remarkable. "I guess that there's something permanently fucked-up about me, like Alison said. And it means I'll end up alone," he said. "Or even if I'm not, that I'll feel alone, which is maybe worse."

"I know what you mean," I said. "But I don't know about permanent. People can always change. Even when they're old. Nothing's unsalvageable, right?"

"You ever see a therapist?" he asked. "Alison was always trying to get me to go."

"Just for a year when I was twelve or thirteen."

"Because of your parents' divorce?"

"Pretty much," I said.

"I heard you can go to one at school for free," he said. "Sometimes I wonder if it'd be good for me to try it out. Uncover those blind spots."

"Everyone's got a blind spot," I said. "Or at least something they prefer not to think about."

144

"What's yours?"

By this point we'd had a number of fun episodes together, but this moment, the two of us talking in a tranquil pocket of the night, felt more exciting, and I was gripped by the same urge for frank disclosure I'd had when I'd told him that my father paid my tuition, the sense that he was a real friend I could confide in after a lifetime of holding people at arm's length.

"If I knew," I said, "then it wouldn't be a blind spot."

He grinned.

"Let's go to the river," he said. "I haven't seen it at night."

We walked through Stuy Town to an exit at Twentieth Street, went over to the FDR Drive, and crossed it to the East River. The water stretched darkly across to Greenpoint. We followed the fencing south along the pedestrian path until Billy stopped and polished off his whiskey.

"Is it dumb if we write our fears in our bottles and throw them in the water?" he asked. "Or is that just a thing girls do after they've been dumped?"

"Littering is a manly activity," I said.

"Yeah, marking your territory," he said. He took out his notepad and pen and tore off two scraps. Using the notepad as backing, he wrote his down, put it in his bottle and screwed the lid on, and handed the pen to me.

I'd never kept a diary, having always been afraid someone might discover and read it, and wasn't accustomed to writing my private thoughts. I copied down what I'd said to Billy and dropped it in my bottle, which still had some whiskey left.

Billy cocked his arm.

"Wait," I said. "If the lids are on, they'll float, right? And don't we want them to go under?"

"I guess." He unscrewed the lid and flung his bottle over the fence, and I did the same. As expected, his traveled farther than mine. The syncopated splashes pierced the smoothly humming sound of the highway traffic behind us before the bottles sank out of sight forever.

"Really appreciate you taking me in," he said as we walked home.

"It always bothered me that I wasn't using that room," I said.

"Not just the apartment," he said. "I thought no one was going to help me out in New York, and it'd be kind of a lonely time that I'd just have to soldier through. Especially those first few weeks in the basement. So, thanks, man."

His first few weeks in the basement, I thought, had been my first six years in Stuy Town.

"Same here," I said.

His first few weeks in the basement, I thought, had been my first six years in Slovenia.

"... he said."

5

There was little suspense in the air leading up to Election Day; everyone expected Clinton to wallop Dole with assistance, once more, from the amusing third-party peculiarity of Ross Perot. Even for Democrats, the event had the wincing anticipation of a lopsided bout between a heavyweight champion and an underfed amateur.

Billy and I made plans to watch the returns together, and the afternoon of the election I shopped for wine, guacamole and chips, and Brie and crackers. On my way back to the apartment, a ruddy-faced older man outside Beth Israel Hospital was having difficulty getting into a taxi, for reasons I couldn't understand. He struggled by the curb until the cabbie lost patience, yelled at him to close the door, and sped off. The man looked at the ground.

"You okay, sir?" I asked him.

He nodded without looking up.

"Do you want another cab?"

"Thank you," he said quietly. I raised my arm and another taxi pulled over.

"I'm sorry," the man said, "but could I ask you for your help first?" Without bending over, he hiked up his pants leg. Above a loose sock was a glinting aluminum rod where there should have been flesh. I felt a queasy stab in my gut.

"It accidentally locked and I can't bend it," he explained. "So I can't reach down to roll up my pants high enough. Could you do it?"

"Yep," I said, my throat dry. I crouched down to bunch and roll up his beige polyester pants leg along the slender prosthetic calf.

"Light's green," said the taxi driver. "Let's go."

"Hold on!" I shouted with a sharpness I never used.

"I just got this," the man said. "I've never had one before. I'm sorry."

"Don't worry about it," I told him. I slowed down my rolling before I reached the knee. "Okay, you can unlock it."

I turned my head away to let him roll up the last bit and adjust something. He tested the movement and said he was ready. I unrolled the material and helped him into the backseat. It was an obvious but nonetheless jarring insight: with the pants down, you never would have known about his missing leg.

"You'll be okay getting out?" I asked. "What if it locks again?"

"I think so," he said. "If I'm sitting down I can roll it up. They told me it just takes some getting used to."

When Billy came home that night from class, I told him about the encounter. "It made me think of your ex-girlfriend's term. Concealable stigma."

"She meant it metaphorically for me," he said.

"Yeah, I know," I said.

The first wave of election results came in, and Clinton took a quick lead. "Shit, forgot my push-ups," Billy said as he tucked into the food spread. "Mind if I do them here?"

I gestured for him to go for it.

"Sorry, I normally do this in my room." He dropped to the floor, facing away from me. There was a robotic snap to his push-ups, like an assembly-line machine repeating the same motion, bored with its own perfection. His deltoids, exposed by the crescent moons of his tank top, rippled as his body rose and fell, and his triceps strained beneath his skin like a swallowed

150

animal wriggling down the body of a python. It's odd that biceps get all the attention; they're bulky appurtenances, window dressing for the vain, whereas triceps are the more graceful muscles, sinewy armor against the world's slings and arrows. I silently counted to fifty before he stopped and, breathing heavily, plopped back onto the couch and gulped down a full glass of Chardonnay.

I asked if he'd voted absentee in Illinois. "I did," he said.

"I guess your vote makes as little difference in Illinois as it would in New York."

"I think of it as a protest vote."

"What do you mean?"

"To let the Democrats know that they can't take Illinois totally for granted."

"You voted for *Perot*?"

"Dole," he said.

I laughed. He didn't.

"You're serious?"

He nodded and bulldozed some guacamole with a chip.

Billy had shown contempt for certain cosmopolitan East Coast values, but I'd assumed he restricted it to the cultural sphere. It occurred to me that he and I hadn't discussed politics directly once, even during a presidential election year, perhaps a sign

151

of the apolitical times, or maybe I'd had an inkling of where he stood and hadn't wanted it to open up a divide between us.

"You look shocked," he said.

I tried to find the least derogatory wording. "I guess I figured that if you write the kind of fiction you do, you're liberal."

"Why?"

"You know. It's just hard to imagine someone . . . I mean, most artists have liberal beliefs."

"What kind of people do you think become artists?" He spoke in the tone of a professor challenging a freshman to reconsider his knee-jerk assumptions.

"I suppose it's people who have something to say, with the talent and discipline to express it, and the empathy to see other viewpoints."

"Sure, that's all true," he said. "And also the people who have enough of a financial cushion to fall back on in case they don't make it. Which means not many people like me."

I looked at the TV for another election update, but it had switched to a Mr. Clean commercial.

"And you really agree with Dole's *entire* platform?" I asked. "Low taxes, big military, pro-life, no social programs — all of that?"

"Of course not," he said. "I'm pro-choice, though I wish people took more responsibility for their actions. The rich should pay higher taxes. We should have a strong military, but we shouldn't be the world's policeman. And some safety-net programs, but not a nanny state where we just give handouts for nothing."

"So you voted for Bush last time?" I asked.

"Nope," he said. "Clinton."

This was almost more staggering than the previous revelation. I held my lowest opinion for independent voters who, after decades of empirical evidence, still couldn't see the high-contrast differences between the two parties, or who fatalistically thought it didn't matter whom we elected anyway.

"Then why'd you change?"

"I didn't." He punctured some oozing Brie and glazed it over a cracker. "*He* fucking did. He's completely in Wall Street's pocket."

"Okay, but you don't think he's doing a good job with the economy, especially compared to Bush and Reagan? The stock market's the highest it's ever been."

Billy laughed. "I don't know a single person from home who's in the stock market. I know lots of people who're on welfare — or *were* on welfare, until he gutted it."

"But that's exactly the Republican platform, gutting welfare," I said, pouncing on the contradiction. "And besides, you just said we shouldn't give handouts for nothing. Clinton's moving to the center because that's where the country is going. What do you want him to do?"

"Grow a fucking pair," Billy said. "If they're both going to screw us, I'd rather go for the guy who at least says what he believes and has real character. Dole got paralyzed from the neck down rescuing someone in World War Two. Clinton spent Vietnam fucking British women as a Rhodes scholar. Who do you think really cares more about sacrificing for his country? The guy's a total phony. If *Dole* was the one who was a serial womanizer and was being investigated for shady real estate deals, Democrats would be up in arms."

The TV flashed to footage of the president voting for himself earlier that day and waving to the cameras with a presumptively victorious smile.

"Clinton puts on a show of being for the little guy, but only if the people in power, like him, don't have to give up anything of real value," he went on.

I thought about mentioning that Clinton, like him, grew up without a father, in a small, economically marginalized town, that he might be a flawed individual but he'd also risen to where he was by dint of his intellect and hard work. But then Billy added, "Just like a lot of the people who vote for him," and I didn't respond.

Billy went to the bathroom, and after he returned I steered the conversation toward school. We stopped watching at nine o'clock, when the election was called for the incumbent.

The week before Thanksgiving I asked Billy if he was doing anything for it. A scheduling quirk due to the holiday had left him without any hours at the bar for the long weekend, he said, so he just planned to read and write.

"You could come home with me," I said. "My aunt and uncle and cousin are coming for dinner, but they're not sleeping over, and we've got a guest room."

"How do you get there?" he asked. "Train or bus?"

"I actually fly. It's just an hour on the Delta Shuttle."

"Oh. Well, I can't afford a plane."

"You can use two of my tickets," I said. "They're transferable."

"How much are they?"

My father bought my tickets for me in discounted blocks of eight at sixty dollars apiece.

"Don't worry about it," I said.

We flew on Thanksgiving morning to avoid the Wednesday mayhem. I sprang for a cab to La Guardia, telling Billy, who wanted to take public transportation, that I would have gotten one without him, too.

At the airport, the metal detector went off when he stepped through the gate, and he immediately looked to me with panic. "I'm sorry," he said to the TSA employee.

"You have to remove your belt, sir," said the security officer.

I said nothing about the plane, not wanting to make him feel self-conscious about his maiden flight. After boarding, he peered around the cabin, examining — but not touching — the overhead compartments, the seat buttons, even the folding tray. He seemed to have a childlike curiosity tempered by adult embarrassment over experiencing this for the first time in his twenties. When we took off, his hands gripped the armrests until the pilot's airborne announcement. He had the window seat and spent most of the hourlong trip gazing out. He tensed up again upon landing and shut his eyes for the final minute until the wheels hit the tarmac.

"By the way," I said as I spotted my mother's Nissan from the passenger pickup area, "I didn't tell my parents you're living with me, in case my great-aunt isn't crazy about the idea. So let's just pretend you live in university housing." My great-aunt wouldn't have minded at this point, but I didn't want word to get back to my father, who would ask if Billy was contributing to the rent.

We climbed into the backseat of my mother's car, and I made introductions as we pulled out of Logan. "Your parents are still there?" she asked after he told her where he was from in Illinois.

"Yep. They're divorced."

"What do they do?"

"My mom works at a dentist's office. And my dad is at a landscaping company," he said, the last job he'd heard of his holding.

"And where are you living in New York?"

His eyes darted over to mine. "University housing," he said.

The white Colonial we'd been in since I was born was in a neighborhood lushly canopied by oaks and Norway maples, whose streets, patrolled by a private security van, had a hushed placidity that suggested such a prophylactic measure was superfluous. Upon entering and removing his shoes, Billy took in the nineteenth-century British oil reproductions decking the foyer. I felt obligated to give him a tour, so I guided him past the antique dishes and Shaker spinning wheel on display in the living room and loitered in the less froufrou spaces, like the TV room, which housed a dusty Zenith set from the mid-eighties and a Nordic-Track skier.

I asked if he wanted to go in to Boston for a few hours before my aunt and uncle, their son, and his fiancée arrived from Connecticut.

"Shouldn't we help your mother with the food?" he asked.

"She's fine," I said.

He squinted. "You sure? She's making Thanksgiving dinner for seven people."

"We'd just get in the way."

"I'd still like to offer."

At his insistence she allowed him to pitch in. I guiltily volunteered, too, and we chopped vegetables for the stuffing at the table. "Billy, could you pass me the broccoli rabe?" my mother asked from the sink. He surveyed the table's cornucopia of autumn vegetables: turnips, rutabaga, sweet potatoes, squash, Swiss chard, and ingredients for the salad. I could tell he wasn't sure what broccoli rabe was and was leaning heavily on the first word for an interpretation.

"I got it," I said, leaning over the table for the bowl.

Once we'd put in enough time in the kitchen, my mother shooed us out, telling us to relax. "Mind if I watch the Lions game?" Billy asked me. He hadn't turned on any sports events in our apartment, but I joined him in the TV room and read the *Boston Globe* while he watched.

"You into the Pats?" he asked.

"More when I was younger," I lied.

"Makes sense. Sorry about eighty-five."

"Eighty-five?"

"Super Bowl Twenty," he said. "Bears-Patriots. Forty-six ten."

"Right," I said.

"I had a poster of the Fridge scoring his touchdown over my bed all of high school." He smiled goofily at the memory. "You guys have a real shot this year with Bledsoe and Martin. And Parcells is the best in the league."

I grunted and went to the kitchen for some water.

"You know who I saw yesterday at Star Market?" my mother said to me. "Michelle

159

Stein. Remember her?"

"Vaguely," I said as I retrieved a glass from the cupboard.

She closed the kitchen door.

"Well, her daughter married a man who got testicular cancer," she said in a quieter voice. "In both sides, apparently. And the sperm they saved before his operation wasn't working with fertility treatments. So they adopted a beautiful little girl from China."

I ran the cold water.

"She said she thinks her daughter loves her even more than if she were her own," my mother continued.

I filled my glass before the water was cold enough for my liking.

"There are several adopted children in her kindergarten, too," she said. "It's apparently much easier to do nowadays, through agencies and what have you."

"I get it." I knocked down the tap. "Good for Michelle Stein's daughter."

I returned to the TV room and the arts section of the *Globe.* Near the end of the game the phone rang, and after a moment my mother said my father wanted to speak with me. We hadn't talked since the semester had started, and any cash infusions I'd needed had been obtained by my leaving him messages on his answering machine when he was at work. I took the cordless into my room and didn't pick up until the door was closed.

"Hi, Dad," I said.

"Hello, there," he said. "Happy Thanksgiving from San Diego." He and my age-appropriate stepmother went there on the major holidays to visit her extended family.

"You, too." I cleared my throat. "How's the weather out there?"

"It got up to about sixty-nine today." He chuckled. "Makes me wonder why we live in Boston."

"I can imagine," I said. "It's been really cold and windy here."

"Your mother tells me you've brought a friend from Columbia home."

"Billy."

"And she says you're enjoying your program?"

I'd told my mother that things were going well in my workshop to prevent her from relaying anything that might make him rethink his tuition payments for an already questionable arts degree. "I am," I said. "Learning and writing a lot. How's work?"

"Busy." He made a little surprised sound, followed by a laugh. "Lisa's nephew just grabbed onto my leg. He likes it when I

161

walk around with him on board." To the boy he said, "One minute, you little barnacle."

I couldn't recall much roughhousing between us growing up; he interacted with the physical world the way he did as a chemical engineer, abstractly and with forethought, through equations and diagrams, rigorously adhering to the scientific method. I once came across a map of the U.S. he'd used for a cross-country trip we'd taken when I was seven, and each leg of the journey was annotated with mileage and estimated travel time.

He took in a deep, summing-up breath. "Well, happy Thanksgiving again."

"See you at Christmas."

"Oh, I didn't tell you," he said. "We're going to Paris, an apartment swap. Lisa's never been. What days will you be back?"

It turned out our schedules didn't overlap. He told me he was sorry, but he'd make certain he was around the next time I was in town.

"Sure thing," I said. " 'Bye, Dad."

"Goodbye," he said.

"Wait." I'd always hated this part in college enough that I'd overlooked it until now, where our few minutes of polite phone conversation resulted in a transfer of funds.

"I forgot, Columbia needs the check for next semester in two weeks."

"Okay," he said as Lisa's nephew implored him to play. "Just leave me a message at home with the details." His phone clattered in its cradle. It occurred to me for the first time that my father might retire to San Diego in a decade or so, and if that happened, it was hard to imagine either of us ever visiting the other.

Back in the TV room, Billy was perched on the edge of the couch at a presumably pivotal juncture in the game, the fans raucous, the clock showing less than a minute left. "What's going on?" I asked.

"Hold on," he said, raising his palm. One of the players was handed the ball and dived into the end zone. "Holy shit!" he exclaimed, leaping to his feet as the crowd deflated. Then he sat down, seemingly embarrassed by his exultation. "Crazy game. How's your dad?"

I hadn't talked about him much with Billy after trading notes that first time. "Fine. He's in San Diego with his wife's family."

"Remind me — did your parents split custody?"

My parents had minimized the rupture they'd created by amicably agreeing that my mother, who had done nearly all the parenting anyway, would retain full custody. My father had broken the news and details of the divorce to me ahead of when they'd planned to tell me. I'd woken up in the middle of the night and gone down to the kitchen for something to eat when I noticed, in the open living room, the dark figure of my father under a blanket on the couch.

"Dad?" I asked.

"Go back to sleep," he mumbled.

"Why are you down here?"

"I had trouble sleeping in the bed."

"But your back hurts when you lie down on the couch."

From his pause — and the tense dinners we'd sat through in recent months, most of the conversation triangulated through me — I knew something was wrong. He sat up and put on his glasses from the coffee table. "Come over here," he said.

I sat by him as he gave me all the usual explanations and assurances: that he and my mother had been having problems lately, that they'd tried their hardest to work things out but nothing was helping, that they loved me and, though it would be painful now, this was the best option for all of us. I had never longed for a sibling as much as at that moment. Older, younger, brother, sister — it didn't matter; I just wanted another person to shoulder the pain with me, to go through exactly what I'd have to go through.

"I know this has been a difficult time for you. And you've been very stoic about . . . everything," he said. "But this has nothing to do with you. This is all between your mother and me."

"I know," I said.

I told Billy that I'd lived with my mother and that my father came in from Boston once a week to take me to dinner.

Billy was still watching the TV. "My mom told me my dad didn't come by for six months after they split up."

"Well, after I went to college, it sort of just became holidays and birthdays," I said.

"Good thing there are mothers," he said as the game cut to a commercial. "Yours is nice."

"Thanks," I said. "She can be sort of meddling."

"Better than not giving a shit," he said.

I wasn't close to these relatives, seeing them just once or twice a year. My cousin, a year my senior, had brought along his fiancée, whom he'd met in medical school at Johns Hopkins. Thomas was puppyishly exuberant in greetings, hiked and biked on weekends in Maryland, ensconced himself in performance fleece, responded to most comments with "awesome" or a variant. The woman he was engaged to was a distaff version of him. Both seemed incapable of self-doubt or -loathing. They hadn't set a date yet, but I dreaded whenever it would be.

At dinner Thomas recounted, almost day by day, the two weeks he'd recently spent in Kenya through a medical aid program tending to villagers who lacked basic healthcare, and flaunted a picture of a little boy hugging him. Then he discussed his and his fiancée's upcoming vacation to Australia over Christmas.

"How about you?" he asked me after he'd indefatigably monologued for a quarter of an hour. "Are you writing a novel?"

"Short stories."

"Nice. What're they about?"

"They're usually about ten to twenty pages long," I said, my stock deflection. No one laughed. "I don't like to bore people with descriptions of them."

"They're really good," said Billy.

"Man, I wish I had time to write. I have a million stories from Kenya alone," Thomas said. "Scratch that — I wish I had time to *read.*"

The next day I took Billy in to Cambridge. "Sorry about my cousin," I said over coffee

166

in Café Pamplona. "I know he's a little much."

Billy tapped his cigarette against the ashtray more than necessary. "He's all right."

"You can say it. I find him really annoying."

"I don't know," he said. "I'm just always amazed people will fly halfway around the world to take care of some Africans when there are plenty of African *Americans* ten minutes away in Baltimore who could use his help."

"Okay, but the Kenyans need the help even more," I said. "You could argue that it makes sense from a utilitarian standpoint."

"Then he could donate the money he spent on his plane ticket directly to the Kenyans. Or if he's going to go there, do the less glamorous work of helping set up a clinic so they can take care of themselves, instead of needing Americans like him to come in and rescue them." His mouth twisted scornfully. "Even if he has the best intentions, *he* wants to be the one to get credit for helping them. He wants the cute picture as a trophy, and it all becomes another fun trip for him to tell a story about. Same as going to fucking Australia."

Despite my own disdain for Thomas,

167

Billy's interpretation seemed far too cynical. But I said, "Maybe." Since the election, I hadn't brought up politics with him. We clearly weren't going to come to any agreement, and it would just be a source of friction.

"Sorry, man," Billy said. "He's your family, and I'm being a dick. Your cousin's trying to fix problems in the world, and I'm sitting at home making up problems for imaginary people."

We spent the rest of the weekend working and hanging out at home. When we were getting ready for the airport on Sunday morning, I couldn't find my Dopp kit. Billy was in the bathroom, but I didn't hear the shower running, so I knocked on the door and asked if it was there.

"Yeah," he said. "Hold on a sec." The shower turned on. "Okay, come in, it's on the toilet," he called.

I opened the door. The sunshine through the window silhouetted his body in profile on the semi-opaque curtain as he stood under the stream. My Dopp kit was on the toilet tank, right next to the shower. I went over for it, and the small gap between the curtain and the wall exposed the muscled curve of his buttocks glazed with water.

I grabbed the Dopp kit and walked out.

6

The week before winter break Billy came to my room and asked if I knew anyone with a car he could pay to borrow. His cousin was getting married that weekend in Pennsylvania, he said, and he hadn't realized how expensive it was to rent a car in New York or take Amtrak; the cost of either would preclude his staying in a motel. I told him I didn't.

"Shit. I guess I'll just take the bus," he said.

"How long's the ride?"

"Longer by bus, like nine hours, but I could take it midnight on Friday and come back Sunday."

"That'll be terrible. Just say you have a lot of work and can't make it."

"I have to go," he said, rubbing his eyes. "It's a family thing. Especially since my grandmother broke her hip and my mom has to take care of her."

169

I considered lending him the money for the rental but knew he'd say no. Then I had a better idea.

"What if I came with you? I could pay for the car and we could split the motel. I wouldn't go to the wedding, obviously."

"Why would you want to spend the whole weekend driving to some shithole town in Pennsylvania?"

"I like road trips," I answered.

He thought about it as he tapped the side of the doorframe. "I could probably sneak you into the wedding after the dinner."

"Cool," I said. "It'll be nice to get out of the city."

I spent the next afternoon making a mixtape on my boom box for the car ride. On Saturday morning we took the subway and bus to JFK, where the rental cars were less expensive, and on the A train sat opposite an ad for the unisex fragrance CK One, featuring Kate Moss and other waifish models of both genders.

"You think she's hot?" Billy asked.

"Kate Moss?" I said. "Of course. She's beautiful."

He grimaced at her picture. "I know I'm supposed to find her attractive, but there's nothing *there*, you know? I like my women to look like women." He nodded at a movie poster next to it for *Romeo + Juliet,* with Leonardo DiCaprio kissing Claire Danes. "She looks almost like him. Or *he* looks like *her.*"

"Girls seem to be into him," I said.

At the airport, as Billy arranged for his car reservation of the cheapest subcompact they had, I asked the desk clerk if it had a cassette player. Only a radio, he informed me; the next model up with one was fifteen dollars more.

"No thanks," Billy said as he signed a form.

"I'll pay for it," I said. "I brought a tape."

"For an extra fifteen bucks? That's like two weeks of tuna fish."

I couldn't tell if he was kidding.

"We're in the car fourteen hours," I said. "It's worth it."

As the one paying for the rental, I prevailed, though perhaps tacking on fifteen dollars to play a single tape was absurd. Still sluggish from our early wakeup and trek to the airport, we didn't talk much while we scrolled by the apocalyptic, smoke-belching horizon of industrial New Jersey onto I-80 for the seven-hour drive. As I would have had to pay a steep surcharge for being under twenty-five, Billy was listed as the only driver, and his earlier comment about not being that skilled was accurate. He was an uncommon combination of slow and reckless, barely nudging above the speed limit on the highway when no one was in front of him yet gunning it in and out of lanes when he had the opportunity to pass another car.

I popped in the tape, and the first track, "Vienna," by Ultravox, started up. "You know this one?" I asked. He didn't. We listened without comment to the New Wave song's heartbeat-mimicking synthetic drums, the manic violin riff, the piano tinkling at the top of the scale as though it were trying to break through the ceiling into an unknown octave. I was still a child when "Vienna" came out and didn't hear it until the song was a decade old, but that was precisely the reason for my attachment to it: I always felt the keenest pangs of nostalgia for pasts not my own, the vinyl soundtracks to other people's formative years, as if those experiences were truer than my own.

"That was really good," Billy said after it faded out. When both sides of the tape were finished, he turned it over and started it up again.

"Say no if you don't want to," he said, "but if you feel like coming to Illinois for part of Christmas break, you're welcome to."

"That'd be fun," I said, already conjuring up what the real-life version of *No Man's Land* might look like.

"I don't know about *fun,*" he said. "There's not much to do. But it'd be cool to show you around anyway."

Our second running of the mixtape ended. We tried the radio, but the few stations we could tune into played only country music.

"Should we do the tape one more time?" Billy asked. I flipped it over, and as "Vienna" began again, the feeling I used to have in college on the occasions I took the bus by myself between New York and Boston returned to me, that melodramatic, romantic rootlessness endemic to the unformed adult in intercity transit, a suspended body roving between geographic points and sealed off from the outside world. Only this time I wasn't alone.

The feeling has gone, only you and I, we and the tinny car speakers harmonized, the wind from the cracked windows frenzying our hair, the December sky widening into an infinite metallic haze as we hurtled westward, Lewis and Clark in a '92 Geo Metro, buzzed from nicotine and caffeine and excitement of the unknown — of that night, our youth, life — *it means nothing to me, it means nothing to me, this means nothing to me,* though the singer was in denial (whenever someone vehemently insists it means nothing to them, it of course means everything), and the final two words of the chorus snuff out his self-delusion and return him to the solid materiality of a time and place he can never escape, even if it no longer exists: *Oh, Vienna.*

From a distance, the old steel town looked plucky and quaint in the waning afternoon light, its skyline studded with smokestacks, steeples, and squat water towers. But as we approached, the redbrick factories were the color of a steak that had been left in the freezer too long; entire portions of some had expired and fallen off, and what remained sat on piles of crumbs. Many had the name of a company inscribed on top followed by the year they were established, presumably with all the hope of a baby's birth, and I found myself wishing this was followed by an en dash and the year they went under to endow them with the dignity of a tomb.

My touristic exhilaration, however, only grew with the majestically grim backdrop. I'd never stayed overnight in a town as bleak as this, an experiential deficit I'd always felt inadequate about for my writing purposes, especially given what was in vogue in contemporary fiction, still under the influence of Raymond Carver's minimalist portraits of blue-collar America.

We pulled in to the motel that was blocked off for wedding guests. Billy had reserved a double room, thinking that meant two beds, but we discovered that it had only a single queen-size bed. No rooms with two beds were available. Ours didn't have a couch, and the motel was out of cots.

"We have one extra room, if you'd like to split up," the clerk said.

"I'll pay for it," I offered.

"That's ridiculous," said Billy. "We'll make do with the one bed."

"You sure?"

"It's too much money otherwise."

We settled into the bare-bones, wall-to-wall-carpeted room that smelled of bleach and cigarette smoke. As Billy showered, I rested my head on a starchy pillowcase and read the *New Yorker.* He dressed in the bathroom and came out in chinos fraying at the cuffs, black dress shoes with cracking leather, a belt with a Pilgrim-style square buckle, a billowy mauve button-down, a cheap paisley tie, and a shoulder-padded gray polyester sports coat fit for a bank branch manager. They had clearly all been picked from thrift (not "vintage") store racks and bins, and yet the chimerical ugliness of the ensemble almost accentuated his handsomeness.

"This look okay?" he asked. "I'm so uncomfortable in this shit."

"It's good. Wait — your shirt collar." It was upturned in the back. He tried to fix it but didn't end up doing anything. "Hold on," I said. I got up and adjusted it myself, the backs of my fingers pressing against his nape.

"Let's take a cab to and from the reception so you can drink," I said before Billy drove to the ceremony on his own. "I'll cover it."

"You don't have to pay for everything, you know," he said.

"It's fine. The cab won't be much."

"It's not just the cab. The car, the motel. It's adding up."

"Really, it's not that expensive," I said. "You're a cheap date."

He looked down at his tie and loosened it a little. "Okay," he said.

I showered and put on my own gray suit, a graduation present from my father given, and seemingly designed with its aggressive squareness, for job interviews that never materialized. When Billy returned to the motel from the church, we took a cab to the reception, held at an Italian restaurant in a strip mall. We set a time to reunite and I found a pizzeria, where I ate a couple of slices and bided my time playing Pac-Man.

"How is it?" I asked when Billy emerged from the restaurant, music spilling out after him. A red polyester carpet runner extended from its entrance to the parking lot.

"Redeemed by my seating arrangement," he said, lighting a cigarette. I'd forgotten my pack and motioned for one. "I'm next to one of the single bridesmaids. And I talked you up to her friend, who's very interested in meeting you. They're staying at our motel, too. It's gonna be a fun night."

"Yeah?" I asked, trying to sound game, though I'd hoped this trip would be a short reprieve from women, our equivalent of a hunting trip, and worried, as always, that his salesmanship was falling on indifferent or soon-to-be-disappointed ears. "That'd be nice. I've had a little dry spell since Claire."

"Don't sweat it," he told me. "You're a good-looking guy. She'll like you."

The customary good feeling that came from being complimented on one's appearance was compounded by Billy's saying it,

177

the same way that praise of my writing from him reverberated more deeply than from anyone else.

We entered the restaurant mid-dessert, some of the guests dancing, others eating cake with plastic forks. The older men were rotund and mustachioed, the women pan-caked in foundation, their hair teased and poufed. Plates stained with red sauce waited to be cleared from the tables, and below the purple bunting that sagged around the room, the walls were festooned with photos of Italian American entertainers: Sinatra, Stallone, De Niro, DiMaggio. Def Leppard's "Pour Some Sugar on Me" wailed on two speakers next to a converted dance floor, above which hung a banner: KAYLEIGH AND BRYAN'S WEDDING!!!

As we drank Budweiser from the open bar, Billy pointed out the bridesmaid — whose toothy good looks evoked the wholesome cheer of a team photo — dancing with her raven-haired and gamine friend who was purportedly interested in me. They caught us staring and waved us over. Billy led me to them through the congested dance floor. I apologized for bumping into people along the way, but he somehow didn't seem to touch anyone; his gait was as though he had a moving airport walkway beneath his feet, boosting him to a glide, while I was encumbered by my luggage.

He introduced me to the bridesmaid, Jessica, and then to Marie, who worked in sales for a pharmaceutical company in Ohio and knew the bride from a small state college in Pennsylvania. She asked if I'd seen *Rent* yet.

"No, but our apartment's close to where it's set," I said.

"God, you're so lucky," she said. "I always wanted to live in New York."

"You should move there."

"And why don't I win the lottery while I'm at it."

"Yeah, it's expensive," I said.

The four of us drank and danced. When the party ended we shared a cab to the motel, all squeezing into the back, and Jessica invited us to their room on the second floor.

"Should we split up now?" Billy whispered as we took the stairs behind them. "You can have our room, I'll go upstairs?"

"I think they want to hang out as a group for a little," I said. "Let's not kill the mood."

Their room had two beds. Jessica brought out a bottle of bourbon and opened a small hexagonal plastic container from her purse that contained two pills, one orange, one purple. "You guys do X?" she asked.

Though Ecstasy had been in heavy circulation at NYU, I had turned all opportunities down after hearing horror stories about the depression hangover.

"I'll do it if you do it," Billy said to me.

I didn't want a repeat with Marie of what had happened with Claire, and I figured it might help me relax. But more than that, I wanted to punctuate our semester with an adventure, something Billy and I would remember for a long time.

"I'm in," I said.

Jessica cut the pills in half using the edge of a barrette's metal clasp. "A little extra for the growing boys." She handed us the slightly larger pieces. "These are weak, so it won't hit too hard. But you'll feel something in a little bit."

We passed around the bourbon, Billy and Jessica sitting on one bed, Marie and I on the other, talking about nothing in particular. "Tonight must be just like a New York nightclub to you," she said. "The restaurant, this motel. So glamorous, right?"

"I think I saw Leonardo DiCaprio back there with Claire Danes," I said.

"No, that was Brad and Gwyneth," she said. "People are always confusing me with her. It's so embarrassing."

"And me with Brad," I said. "I hate it. It's

180

like, of all the movie stars, *him*?"

I wondered why I was generating and laughing at such dumb humor, and then, though I must have been feeling it for some time, I registered what was happening.

"Shit," Marie said, looking euphorically surprised. "I think it's hitting me."

"Me too," said Billy. "Fuck. It's like I'm inside a . . . bubble of honey."

We all privately savored the tingly sensations. I couldn't believe I'd passed up this experience in college. How many other things I'd missed out on.

"I can't get over it," Jessica broke the silence. She stroked the swollen band of Billy's torqued neck muscle for what seemed to be a minute without speaking again.

"You're so completely beautiful," she said. "Every single part of you."

They made out with the uninhibited fervor of teenagers. She unbuttoned his shirt and threw it on the floor, leaving him in his tank top. I watched for a moment before I saw Marie smiling at me. We kissed, her tongue a living autonomous thing against mine. Sweat pebbled my forehead, but it felt good, almost refreshing, and for once in my life I didn't care. Maybe this was how normal people were all the time: unguarded, receptive to joy, life as a series of gardens to wander through, not thorns to sidestep.

Jessica turned off a lamp and the room darkened. As my pupils adjusted, I could see her and Billy lying down on their bed.

"Let's go downstairs," Billy whispered.

"In a minute," Jessica told him. "Marie, come here."

"Hold on," Marie said to me. She moved over to their bed. Jessica sat up and caressed her face.

"That feels good," Marie said, her eyes lidded, lips parted in an indolent half smile. They kissed. Billy and I watched, mesmerized, as the stuff of so many male fantasies unfolded before us. Jessica returned to Billy, their energies redoubled, before switching over to Marie, then back and forth, Billy then Marie then Billy then Marie, until there was barely any space between them, a three-headed body taking pleasure of itself.

I was as aroused as I'd ever been. The drug had liberated us; it didn't matter who was touching whom because no one was only themselves, our bodies had indistinct borders, we were sexual internationalists. This is life, I thought — I was experiencing life right then at its most wanton and decadent, a worthy moment to preserve in the amber of memory.

Except I wasn't part of it; I was just a spectator.

I swung my legs off the bed, traversed the carpeted gorge to join their huddle, and, after kissing Marie, brought my mouth to Jessica's, tasting her saliva that had mingled with the others', her mouth warm with their collective heat. My eyes closed, I reached out to touch Marie and felt the warmth of skin.

Then the mattress bounced as Billy got off. I'd been touching him.

"Come back," said Jessica.

He stood there looking at the three of us, his expression not fully legible in the darkness.

"I'm going to bed," he announced.

"What's wrong?" Jessica asked.

Before any of us could stop him, he snatched his shirt from the floor and the sports coat he'd thrown on a chair. "Don't go," Jessica called out, but the door shut behind him.

His abrupt departure was disconcerting. In the span of some thirty seconds, we'd gone from four young lotus-eaters embarked on a carnal adventure to three people in a motel room, confused about what had just transpired and what to do next.

"What the fuck was that?" Jessica asked.

It had been too dark for them to see what had happened. "I'll go find out," I told them.

"Ask if he wants me to come down," she said.

I waited ten minutes outside our room to give him time to cool off, thinking about what I should say. It was an innocent mistake; my eyes had been closed, everyone was huddled together, the drugs and alcohol had disoriented me; he was overreacting to a meaningless slipup.

The only light in the room came from a missing louver in the blinds that imprinted a neon bar from the motel sign on the carpet. Our bed and the bathroom were empty.

"Billy?"

"Here," came his monotone from the far side of the bed. He was on the carpet, facing the wall, with a pillow and the thin top blanket.

"What're you doing down there?"

"Bed's uncomfortable."

"The floor can't be better," I said.

He didn't respond. I sat on the bed, preparing to talk.

"Hey, I'm really sorry about kissing Jessica," I told him, abandoning the speech I had planned. "I thought we were all sort of . . . I didn't mean to horn in on anything."

"It's fine," he said.

"I wasn't trying to steal her, if that's what you were thinking. I'd never do that."

"It's fine," he repeated. "I'm going to sleep. Okay?"

"But I should go on the floor and you should take the bed."

"I'm good," he said with a blunt finality.

I got up to brush my teeth, and when I returned he was lightly snoring. The Ecstasy was now making me tired, but I couldn't fall asleep, and a mysterious, intermittent scratching sound made my insomnia worse; I knew I'd be up for hours. I kept my eyelids open, hoping they'd droop with exhaustion. But I could soon see well in the dark, and it seemed as though all my other senses were performing above their normal functioning for the most undesirable of objects. By four in the morning the unadorned walls, the crunchy sheets, the tang of smoke no longer resonated as a romantic embodiment of red-blooded Americana. This was just a dismal way station for people with nowhere else to stay.

When I woke in the morning, Billy was already dressed and zipping up his toiletries case.

"Hey, man," he said. "Mind if we get out of here soon? It's a long drive."

As we set out on I-80, I tried to formulate a better explanation for the previous night, or at least make a joke about the Ecstasy's effects on my hand-eye coordination. But my resolve to address it eroded with each passing mile of silence.

"Did your mom teach you to drive?" I asked.

"Why? You think I drive like a woman?"

"No." I laughed in case he thought I was insulting him. "I just assumed your dad wasn't around when you were old enough."

"Yeah," he said. "My mom did."

"So did mine," I told him.

We stopped speaking again. A blockade had sprung up between us, all from a stupid error I'd made. In our rental car on the interstate, hundreds of miles from anyone I knew, I had the sudden impulse to tell him something about myself I'd never told anyone.

"How'd you chip your tooth?" I asked.

"Hmm?" he said, as if it were something he'd forgotten about despite his habit of running his tongue over it. "Oh. Basketball game freshman year. I took an elbow."

"I had a friend in college who chipped a tooth and got it capped, and now she's always worried about breaking it when she eats anything hard."

"My mom said it would build character if I lived with it."

"Did it?"

"She said that every time something went wrong. Probably an excuse to not pay for a dentist."

"Well, now she works at one, so you could probably get it done for a discount," I said.

"I've gotten used to it," he said.

I prattled on with a story about my sadistic childhood dentist, trying to distance myself from thinking about what I'd almost said earlier.

"So what airport should I fly into to get to you?" I asked when we drove by a billboard advertising tours for a cave. "I could rent a car there and drive in if you're far from it."

He changed lanes to pass the car ahead of us. "Actually," he said as he accelerated, "I was thinking this isn't a great time to visit. My mom needs help with my grandmother."

"Yeah, of course," I said.

We were quiet again. I pressed Play on the stereo, and the tape started on "Vienna."

"Okay if we turn it off?" Billy asked within a minute. "I'm really tired, and I just want to focus on the driving."

"I'll take it out so we don't forget it," I said, ejecting the tape. "It's yours. If you want it."

"Thanks, man," he said and, returning to the right-hand lane, remained at eighty-five miles per hour, the speed at which we rode in near silence the rest of the way home.

■ ■ ■ ■

1997

■ ■ ■ ■

7

I returned after New Year's to Manhattan in its holiday hangover, the streets littered with the carcasses of Christmas trees and storefronts advertising January sales. I'd left for Massachusetts the day after we returned from the wedding, and Billy and I hadn't spoken during the vacation; I figured a little break from each other would smooth over the friction that had developed from the motel. Things could get claustrophobic in an apartment, even a spacious two-bedroom.

He was typing at his desk when I stepped into the apartment. "Hey, man," he said. "How was your vacation?"

"Good," I said. "Or as good as it can be, living with my mom. You?"

He smiled. "Same."

"You want to do something tonight?" I called as I dropped my bags in my room.

"Sure," he said. I was relieved; he seemed

happy to see me.

"What do you want to do for dinner?" I asked a few hours later. "We could go out, if you don't feel like cooking. My treat."

"I'm kind of in the zone," he said, nodding at his monitor. "I might just heat up some soup and work through dinner. Maybe we could rent a movie or something? I want to wake up early."

"Cool," I said. "I'll go find something."

At Blockbuster I selected *Dead Man Walking.* I'd seen it in the theater when it came out, and it had, like *Field of Dreams,* made me tear up by the end, one of the few films to have that effect. I brought back Chinese food for myself and we watched the movie. Halfway through, Billy stood up. "I'm dead tired," he said.

"Dead man standing," I said.

He didn't acknowledge the joke. "I'm going to bed. You keep watching."

"We've got it for two nights. We can finish it tomorrow."

"I'm working tomorrow night. I'm getting some extra hours now."

"Well, we could finish it during the day."

A sigh, though not from fatigue.

"I'm not that into it," he said.

Billy and I had signed up in November to

be in the same workshop for the spring, the one class we shared. Our new professor was Robert Stockton, a fiftysomething fire hydrant of a man who had published three cult novels in a prodigious burst of creativity in the late nineteen-seventies and early eighties — the first about Vietnam grunts (he had served a tour of duty), another about high school football (he had played), the last about a divorced alcoholic writer (of course) — and nothing since. Both of his marriages were to other writers whose careers now surpassed his own. As with Sylvia, his last fifteen years of miserly production, rather than making him come off as over the hill, had only gilded his mystique, and the inevitable rumor was that he was grinding away at a thousand-page magnum opus.

"Call me Stockton," he boomed in a gravelly voice in the first workshop, a nomenclature I already knew would be too martial and athletic for me to deploy without embarrassment. "Well, that sounds like a horseshit opening to *Moby-Dick,* doesn't it?" Some students laughed. It sounded like a line he used for every new class.

Billy submitted a new chapter of *No Man's Land,* and Stockton's hosannas made Sylvia's reverence for his work seem like timid approval.

"Now *that's* how you write dialogue," he said after Billy had read aloud the first page. "Terseness, omissions, inarticulateness. Less is more, Hemingway's iceberg. None of this flowery shit I see all over the place these days, where the characters tell you every fucking thing on their minds like they're talking to their shrink about how Mommy didn't hug them enough. In real life, people don't say what they want to say. A lot of times they don't even *think* it."

Instead of freeing us to play darts on our own after class, he all but dragooned everyone for "drinks with Stockton," not at the bar we were used to, but an Irish pub several blocks uptown where, upon his entrance, he and the bartender engaged in a performative and not all that clever show of affectionately insulting each other with Anglo and Irish slurs.

Over rounds of Scotch, Stockton machine-gunned us with his pontifications on literature and life: "No one has more than half a dozen good books in them." "Don't get married, or at least don't get married until you've been published." "Make sure your first book is deckle-edged or you'll never get any respect." "Don't ever read a best-seller, it's automatically middlebrow horse-

194

shit. The critical darlings are even worse — they're the effluvium from cynical trends, no one actually enjoys reading them, and they'll poison your own work by fooling you into thinking this is what's good. Only read the classics and the stuff no one else has been paying attention to the last decade." (This last piece of advice seemed quite self-serving.)

"You know what ruined the country?" he asked rhetorically, since no one else was saying much. "Abolishing the draft. You're all removed from real suffering, your own and other people's. Someone else does the dirty work while you watch movies about tornadoes and space aliens. It's made your generation a bunch of epicene candy-asses."

He went on to deride the state of contemporary fiction as "effete, pseudo-intellectual crap by Ivy League boys who think throwing around Marxist jargon makes them revolutionaries." One would think his curmudgeonly attacks would have repelled everyone, and a few people did trickle out, but a small circle of students, all young men, found everything that came out of his mouth fascinating and hilarious. A couple of them were guys Billy and I hadn't met in the fall: Adam, lanky and shaggy-haired and Southern Californian, devotee of ringer

T-shirts and owner of a wallet attached by a chain to his billowy jeans, and husky Matt, who wore oversized horn-rimmed glasses and a bushy black beard over a perpetually flushed face, as if he'd just berated an underling (he did, in fact, possess the loudest speaking voice of anyone I'd ever encountered, a sonic event capable of being clearly heard from the bar's restroom).

"You've got work, right?" I asked Billy when Stockton went up for his fourth drink. "Want to get out of here?"

"I can be a little late," he said, and he stayed another half hour before we took the train downtown.

Billy's additional hours at the Eagle's Nest stretched to a full shift on Thursday nights, which put an end to our "Must See TV" tradition. He spent more time working at the Columbia library, and when he was home he kept to his room. He still cleaned the apartment faithfully on Sundays, but our shared dinners became less frequent.

When I asked if he'd take a look at my first workshop story of the semester before I submitted it, he took it into his room and came out an hour later. He'd edited the majority of the sentences on the first page, but after that had done so only sporadically.

"So most of the problems are at the very beginning?" I asked.

"You found your footing after that," he said.

Without him around as much, I picked up the social slack with the college friendships I'd let lapse in the fall. The conversations, usually over happy hour, hewed to a script: there was the recitation of what had happened in our lives since our last encounter, the play-by-play of a recent office kerfuffle, the PG-13 recapping of amorous adventures. Chris was planning to relocate to Los Angeles to pursue a career as a film editor. Tim was moving in with his girlfriend. Eliza had worked for a federal judge last summer and expected a clerkship upon graduation from law school. They were transitioning to adult lives while I stretched to give mine a dim aura of import: I had been writing short stories, the term itself sounding slight; workshop had been a little rocky but it was good for my growth; I'd had a couple of hookups, nothing serious.

I still stopped by the Eagle's Nest once in a while but would rarely stay for more than one drink. Billy was busier while bartending, thanks to the presence of more female patrons; his reputation must have spread. He started bringing them home after his

197

shifts, too, privileging proximity over concerns about being a discourteous roommate. The first time it happened I was already in bed and was woken up as they stumbled into the apartment. Through my door I heard the barely stifled giggles of people who are deriving enormous pleasure from breaking a mandated silence, as Billy and I had done during the snapping poet's reading. I had trouble falling back asleep, and an hour later got up to pee. When I stepped into the hall, the rhythmic creaking of Billy's bed frame greeted me from behind his door with a contrapuntal feminine moan. I retreated to my room and waited until it was quiet again.

My story Billy had lightly edited, "Ill Humor," was workshopped. It was about a man who bitterly sells ice cream out of a truck to spoiled middle schoolers who torment him until he laces their treats with powerful laxatives. When the police connect the crime to him (he accidentally leaves a bit of packaging in one of the ice cream cones, and they trace the product's purchase at the neighborhood drugstore) and knock on the front door to his home, he attempts to flee through the back — but a chronic limp, exacerbated by the cramped conditions inside his truck, prevents him from escaping.

After Stockton apologized for his lateness ("Lynch is in town," he said, without explaining who that was; "I believe it was the *third* bottle of the eighty-two Bordeaux that did us in"), he mutely presided as the class tossed butter knives of criticism my way. I pretended to take notes but instead lost myself in a patch of late-afternoon sunlight spangled like a leopard's spots from the shifting shadows of branches outside and recalled something an English professor had said during a college lecture, that boredom wasn't "invented" until the eighteenth century — 1732 was the first known instance of *ennui* — and that we were living through its golden age, in that we had more leisure time than any previous civilization and also more stimuli, but when we were deprived of those stimuli, it invariably catalyzed boredom because our atrophied minds were unaccustomed to self-entertainment, which fed a vicious cycle of seeking more distractions to evade the terror of thinking.

Billy didn't speak once.

"What really bothered me about this guy," Stockton finally weighed in, "isn't that he gives the kids laxatives. As everyone knows,

I'm the strongest proponent around of poisoning children." He paused for sycophantic laughter. "It's that he's constantly complaining to the reader about his limp, how much every little step hurts, as a setup to the climax where he can't run. Jake's cock is blown away in the war in *The Sun Also Rises,* and he barely mentions it. That's how a real wounded hero acts. All fiction" — this was one of Stockton's verbal trademarks, to carve in stone what *all fiction* was about — "is ultimately about the character showing us — *not* telling us — 'Here's how my life is hard.' If you do your job right, the reader believes it, and feels his pain. For all his bitching and moaning about it, this guy's isn't hard enough."

"Neither is Jake's," said Adam.

"I'll handle the jokes, Adam," Stockton said with a paternally proud smile. I returned my attention to the piebald sunlight.

Billy had a rare Thursday night off from the Eagle's Nest, and I knocked on his door to tell him *Friends* was starting. We hadn't watched it together since December. He was reading *Jesus' Son,* likely for his Contemporary American Fiction class, also taught by Stockton. "I think I'm through with those shows," he said.

"Really? Even *Seinfeld*?"

He closed the book on his chest. "All shows, period. They're just about yuppies, made by yuppies, for yuppies. What's the other idiotic one everyone talks about at school? On MTV, the documentary?"

"*The Real World.*"

"*The Real World,*" he scoffed. "That's what reality is to people who spend their lives watching TV."

"They are pretty vapid," I agreed.

"They're worse than just vapid," he said. "They supposedly solve the problem of loneliness by showing you a bunch of actor 'friends' who get together in their apartments or coffee shops for these little adventures that make us forget about our lives for half an hour." It sounded like something our workshop professor might say over his third Scotch, which he may well have; I'd begun skipping the drinks-with-Stockton sessions. "But all they're really doing is isolating viewers in their own apartments. You get lonely, so you watch people on TV having fun together without you, which makes you more lonely, so you watch more TV alone."

The glazed-eyed afternoons of my youth had been spent gorging on reruns of formulaic sitcoms, *WKRP in Cincinnati* and *Diff'rent Strokes* and *Three's Company,* the ensemble casts more memorable to me now than my elementary school friends. The one I watched most religiously was *The Facts of Life,* not because I found it all that funny, and I was still too young to lust after its bevy of teenage actresses, but for the slide into its warm bath of pigtails and schoolgirl uniforms and bunk-bed gossip, the glimpse into an era just seconds before mine and the exhilarating surveillance of a pubescence far from my own. I didn't reveal my fandom to anyone at school; the boys were in thrall to the guns and armored vehicles of *The A-Team* and *Knight Rider,* and the disclosure that I preferred the interpersonal dramas of a girls' boarding school would have permanently exiled me. As if they were old acquaintances I'd lost touch with, I perked up whenever I was in line at the supermarket and an actor from one of these shows landed on a tabloid cover with a mug shot. I wasn't that interested, though, in the people who everyone knew had gone into tailspins in their careers and personal lives, the predictable result of stardom or even semi-stardom. I was more curious about the ones who'd simply disappeared, who had enjoyed bit parts on reasonably successful shows for years, seen by millions each week, and then were never heard from again —

character actors sidelined twice over.

I thought about repeating my college professor's ideas on boredom but worried Billy would find something to criticize about that, too. I was about to close the door and watch TV alone but, unable to stop myself, said, "Sort of rough workshop for me yesterday."

"Mm-hmm," he mumbled as he read.

"I was wondering why you didn't say anything in class about my story."

He peered at me over his book. "What do you mean?"

I felt pathetic for bringing it up, but now that I'd started, I couldn't retreat. "I don't know," I said. "You used to defend me when everyone else was piling on. But you didn't talk once yesterday."

He ran his fingers through his hair, twisting it into a samurai's topknot before letting it cascade down.

"So, what did you really think? Were they right?"

He yawned for an extended beat. The mildness of the gesture on his supine frame was reminiscent of a lion doing the same on the veldt. "No," he said.

I waited for him to elaborate, but he didn't. "Just 'no'?"

"Maybe it was a little too" — he paused,

not because it looked like he was trying to come up with the right word, but because he was trying not to offend me — "cerebral."

"I didn't realize 'cerebral' was a pejorative," I said, aware that I was being oversensitive and childish, pestering him for validation, the worst kind of writerly reaction to criticism.

He deliberated for even longer this time. "Look, you —" The old woman's shouts erupted from next door, something about her caretaker not flushing the toilet enough or flushing it too much.

"You know the technical ins and outs of writing fiction as well as anyone," he continued after she quieted down. "You give the most analytical feedback in class. I think what people are pointing to is that you're missing something."

I now regretted bringing it up even more, but my neediness wasn't the reason. I was afraid of finding out what others really thought of me — yet I also couldn't resist picking the scab. "I'm missing something?"

"Or more like something from you is missing in the work," he said. "Who you really are doesn't always show up in your writing. And what everyone's saying is that this other stuff you put in — plot twists and allusions and whatnot — is kind of evasive."

"So I should be 'bleeding onto the page,' like that ridiculous poet?"

"No, man, you don't have to be like him," Billy said, but it was clear what he was telling me, the same thing my classmates and professors had been hinting at all year: I was merely an accountant-like practitioner of the form who lacked an artist's soul — or, like my great-uncle, I couldn't show it. Even the obnoxious poet had something over me.

Billy spanned his temples with his thumb and pointer finger and closed his eyes. "Sorry. I'm tired. I can barely think."

"No, I'm sorry," I said. "It's not your responsibility."

I dawdled by the door. Though it had now been over a month, I thought again of apologizing for what had happened in the motel.

"How is that?" I asked, motioning toward *Jesus' Son.* "I never read it."

"It's good," he said. "I've got to get through it tonight, actually, if you don't mind closing the door."

It was a mild January with little snow, and I got in the habit of going for afternoon walks through Stuy Town. I'd wander the looping paths and service vehicle ramps past children and their parents on the playgrounds, the winter-bald patches of lawn, the commanding fountain in the central concrete oval, listening to my Discman and weaving through the matching buildings.

I made these minor-radius perambulations under the guise of gathering termite-art material, the flâneur casting his gimlet eye on the city, and at the outset of each walk I hoped for some inspiration derived from communion, to be subsumed into the architecture and activity and pedestrians. But everyone else was walking to somewhere or engaged in their own pursuits, a member of society coursing through their daily circuits, and the feeling that I was different from them all — not in any obvious way, not to a degree that anyone would notice — would come back twofold by the end, and all my literary imagination ended up hitching on were ideas for more fantastically plotted stories.

As evening set in, buttery rectangles of light in the windows flickered with the cool alien glow of televisions. I sometimes ventured beyond the confines of Stuy Town, passing a ground-floor apartment on Ninth between First and A, where a fishbowl window exposed a warmly lit tableau out of turn-of-the-century Scandinavia, with a multitude of small wooden clocks, a roll-top desk, and a typewriter at which, on occasion, sat a man with a wizard's beard — another man out of his time's joint, though happily, it seemed.

The deeper my excursions into Alphabet City, the more I noticed people with observable illnesses or afflictions, skin conditions, the wheelchair-bound. Something lurched inside me each time. As a response, when I saw certain walkers from a distance, even those bundled up in outerwear, I developed a reflexive anticipation of a physical defect in them. My predictions never panned out, but I still seized up as I passed them, afraid to look but unable to turn away.

Form rejections for "Camp Redwood" had dribbled into the mailbox through the fall and winter, the sight of my handwriting on the self-addressed envelopes triggering a Pavlovian deflation of the ego. So when I stood in the lobby and opened up the letter from one of the last university journals I'd yet to hear from, I braced for yet another dismissal:

Thank you for giving us the opportunity to read "Camp Redwood." The other editors and I were quite taken with your work, and if it is still available, we would be pleased to publish it in our spring issue.

" 'Camp Redwood' is getting published," I told Billy when we crossed paths in the kitchen, showing just a fraction of my elation.

"Congrats, man," he said. I'd expected a bigger reaction, or even just a question about it, but he finished cranking open his can of tuna fish and glopped mustard onto the disc.

"It wouldn't have happened without your help," I said. "The Karl Malone to my Robert Stockton."

"John Stockton. Robert's our professor."

"I meant John," I said.

Columbia's library didn't carry the journal, but I planned to put one of the contributor copies that I would receive in its magazine rack so everyone could see what had become of the story they'd spurned.

8

I was reading on the couch on an early Sunday evening when Billy came out in his jacket.

"Going to Gristedes?" I asked, taking out my wallet to give him money for a box of cereal.

He paused by the door. "Heading out."

"Eagle's Nest?"

"Actually, Adam and Matt are having a little Super Bowl thing."

"Oh," I said. "I forgot it was the Super Bowl tonight."

He jingled his keys in his pocket. "Want to come?"

"Why not." I said. "I've had my fill of Pynchon for the day."

We arrived in Morningside Heights and let ourselves into Matt and Adam's un-locked apartment. Three other guys from our program I hadn't met were also there, eating pizza and Buffalo wings on a futon and folding chairs.

"How *you* doin'?" Adam said to Billy in the mock-seductive voice of Joey from *Friends*.

"How *you* doin'?" Billy parroted, despite having belittled the show to me.

"You're just in time for the society of the spectacle, pigskin edition," said Matt.

Luther Vandross sang the national anthem. Backup dancers fluttered winged capes in red, white, and blue. "Is the Super Bowl held in America?" Matt asked. "I can't tell."

"I believe it's in France," Adam said. "This all seems very Parisian."

"What's the spread again?" one of the new guys asked.

"Packers by fourteen," said Adam. "Over/under's forty-nine."

"I've got ten bucks on the over with Matt," Billy said.

"Me too. You want to get in on a bet?" Adam asked me. "Or are you a neutral observer?"

Before I could reply, Billy said, "He's a Patriots fan."

"Nice," Adam said, reaching over Billy to high-five me. "They're my team, after the Chargers. We can do a prop bet instead. I've got the whole list." He reviewed a small-font printout of bets with odds. "Want to do . . . who scores the first touchdown by the Patriots?"

I tried to read the list in his hands but couldn't make it out. "Who are the options?"

"Everyone. Just give any name, and I'll tell you the odds."

I looked at the TV for help, but it was on a commercial break. "Parcells?" I said.

He looked confused before smiling. "That's funny," he said. "Is there even a bet for the coaches? Oh — which color Gatorade gets dumped on them."

"I'll sit this one out," I said and shut up after that, determined to follow along without further exposing my ignorance. Touchdowns were scored, passes intercepted, commercials mocked, flatulence attributed to dietary sources. I wished I hadn't come; this wasn't the place for me. The halftime show opened with a performance by Dan Aykroyd, Jim Belushi, and John Goodman, in Blues Brothers garb, butchering "Soul Man."

"The horror, the horror," Adam said.

"It wasn't enough that the NFL exploits black men for its sport," Matt said. "It also had to plunder their culture with the worst possible ambassadors of whiteness."

"Their first choice was David Duke singing 'Dixie,' " said Adam.

"And yet," Matt said sardonically, "aren't we the ones being exploited most of all, by relinquishing our agency for four hours to our corporate masters?" He asked if we minded if he changed the channel. No one objected, so he roamed around and stopped on the volleyball scene from *Top Gun,* the oiled torsos of tanned flyboys glistening on-screen. "Good counterprogramming to large men jumping on each other," he said.

"You see that movie where Tarantino has a monologue about how *Top Gun* is all about Maverick's struggle with his homosexuality?" one of the guys asked.

"Not that there's anything wrong with that," said another.

Billy and Adam won their bets with Matt well before the game was over. The two victors cheered and hugged. "I love you, man," Adam said after their clench, parodying the Bud Light commercials. My alienation over not appreciating sports was surpassed only by this, a scene I'd witnessed many times over the years, mostly in bars: men boisterously celebrating the outcome of a game to which I was indifferent, athletics spectation and participation being the only times society encouraged this level of physical contact between males.

I'd been quiet nearly the entire game. I felt like the younger sibling who forces his older brother to let him tag along, then stands by mutely like a useless appendage.

"You guys ever hear Noam Chomsky talk about going to a football game when he was in high school?" I asked the group during a lull, recalling a documentary clip from *Manufacturing Consent* I'd seen in a college seminar and thinking the Chomsky reference might ideologically appeal to Matt. "He wondered why he was supposed to care about who won, since he wasn't friends with anyone on the team. And he realized that organized sports are training for irrational jingoism and submission to authority. You cheer for a team just because you grew up in their town or you go to —"

Everyone roared at something in the game.

"Oooh," Matt said, sucking in his breath through gritted teeth. "And football players don't wear cups."

"Remember when we were little, kids were always like, 'That's *gotta* hurt'?" said Adam. "But, seriously, that's got to hurt."

"Talk about getting 'sacked,'" one of their friends said with air quotes.

"Sorry, what were you saying?" Matt asked. "About Chomsky?"

"Never mind." I went to the bathroom then loitered by their bookshelf for the rest of the game, skimming a dog-eared copy of *Infinite Jest* and some of their magazines. It was harder back then to look occupied while by yourself in a social setting; any nearby prop had to do. I ended up poring over *George* magazine's election issue from the fall with Barbra Streisand on the cover as Betsy Ross.

"Matt's a pretty smart guy," I said to Billy on the subway home. "He seems very political."

"He's one of the leaders in the union," Billy said.

"What union?"

"The grad student union."

"You've been going?" He nodded. "Since when?" I asked.

"Whenever that guy told us about it in the bar."

"Does it actually affect us, or is it more for the PhDs?"

"A little for master's students, mostly for PhDs. But, you know," he said, making an ironic fist, "solidarity."

It was such a small piece of information to withhold from me, but I nevertheless felt betrayed.

"Well, thanks for bringing me," I said.

He took a paperback of *Blood Meridian* out of his jacket pocket. I didn't have any reading material.

"No problem," he said.

I decided to make an appearance at a drinks-with-Stockton session, hoping the atmosphere had changed. It hadn't; the regular scrum around him still listened wide-eyed to his pronouncements. After buying a second drink, I noticed Billy wasn't there. Someone said they thought they'd seen him leave.

He was, once again, trying to duck me. I decided it was time to talk to him. I would ask him point-blank what was wrong, and if he equivocated, tell him that if it had anything to do with the motel room, then he'd simply misread the situation. On the downtown train, I replayed the part of the episode that had upset him, but this time I became a little aggrieved: on top of his misinterpretation of the events, Billy had probably expected me to stay on my side of the room, a passive onlooker, while he had all the fun.

When I opened the door to the Eagle's Nest, Adam and Matt were at the bar, chatting with Billy and scuttling my plans. They all traded quick looks when I approached.

" 'Sup, dude?" Adam said, a word he abused and one I've always thought that, rather than a term of affection, carries an undercurrent of aloofness, an implication that the two speakers will never be close and thus never have to refer to each other by name.

"Drinks with Stockton kind of petered out," I said. "What brings you down to our neck of the woods?"

"Buybacks on bottom-shelf Scotch," Adam said.

"Shh," Billy said, putting a finger over his smiling lips.

"And," said Matt, clapping a hand on Adam's shoulder, "we're celebrating the imminently — and eminently — published author of 'The Hiker.' "

Adam's story, which we'd workshopped the first class of the semester, was about a hiker who sleeps with a girl he encounters on the Appalachian Trail, only to find in the morning that she's absconded with all his belongings, the type of sophomoric, barstool-vernacular soliloquy, invariably written in the unreflective present tense, that, in my experience in creative writing classrooms, only young men produce.

"Congratulations," I said. "What journal?"

"The *Atlantic Monthly*," Adam replied. Thinking he was joking, I waited for the real, less impressive answer. But he didn't crack a smile; he'd even stated it plainly, as though he didn't want to appear boastful. Had it been Billy, I wouldn't have minded at all, would have been happy that good taste prevailed and true talent had received its due. Adam's achievement was salt in the wounds of everyone else who was failing to get published, a reminder that, despite our necessary faith in order and rationality, the universe was unfair and everything was a fluke.

"That's incredible," I said, meaning it more literally than complimentarily.

"I heard you're getting something published, too. Congrats."

"Thanks." I saddled up onto the stool next to him. "Let me buy you guys a round of top-shelf Scotch."

"You don't have to," he said.

I asked Billy for four glasses of the Scotch brand with which we'd toasted his moving in with me. "That's actually our most expensive one," Billy said, looking at the twenty-dollar bill I took out. "I can't really get away with buybacks for it."

"That's fine," I said and slid over my credit card, having overreached and become the pathetic hanger-on who has to buy his friendships. I asked Adam how he'd submitted his piece, what the editorial process entailed, when it would come out. I didn't have to fake my deferential curiosity, though I still couldn't believe it: Adam, who wrote stories about men furtively masturbating to women they saw on the subway (the other one he'd workshopped), had been endorsed by an established arbiter of literary excellence — and Billy now had an empirical reason to admire him as a writer.

As Billy got hung up with another patron, Adam responded to my questions without arrogance or even insincere humility, chalking its acceptance up to the luck of the slush pile, and politely asked about my own accepted story. When we finished our Scotches and Billy returned to us, Adam set his tumbler down on the bar with a conclusive thunk and smiled broadly to indicate that the conversation was done.

"Well," I said with stagy weariness, "I should get going."

"Stick around for a little," Billy said. "You want to do some coke with us?"

I downplayed my surprise at his invitation. "Sure."

"So, the guy only sells eight-balls," he said. "And it's one-fifty. I've only got twenty on me."

Matt, Adam, and I had fifty between us.

"We're eighty short," Billy said.

There was a silence.

"My bank's down the block," I said. "I could make up the difference."

"You sure?" Billy asked.

"It's fine," I told him.

"Thanks, man, that's cool of you," he said. Adam and Matt chimed in, their excessive gratitude making it clear they weren't going to pay me back. I felt like a fool as I went to the ATM, but if I went home, I'd look cheap. Just this once, I told myself, I'd pony up. I withdrew the money, and the receipt notified me that I had a balance of just forty-six dollars. I hadn't noticed the dwindling numbers these past few months as I'd run through the check my father had written me at the start of the school year.

I returned to the bar and handed the cash to Billy. After he completed the transaction, we took turns in the grotty restroom. The euphoria of the stimulant soon curdled into irritability over how blithely Billy had used me for my money — not just that night, but ever since he'd moved in. And though he almost always asked if I was sure about paying for him, he never put up much of a fight, happily enjoying the trickle-down microeconomics in which capital from my father ultimately flowed down to him.

I left the bar before the others did, detouring through Alphabet City's scraggly, undeveloped lots and utilitarian storefronts, a lone vendor selling kimchi-relish hot dogs, street murals of Newport cigarettes and the 1994 World Cup, a spray-painted request on a dumpster to PLEASE HIDE YOUR DRUGS ELSEWHERE THANK YOU ☺, another on a wall that said FUCK FASCIST GULIANI [sic], and crossed into the East Village as the coke wore off. A light rain began to fall. The buildings of the neighborhood were all a similar shade of graphite, a monochromatic lineup of gravestones against a funereal sky. In the distance, the Empire State Building's white lights were dimmed by a shawl of fog.

The rain subsided when I reached the courtyard behind my apartment, where the pavement shimmered with the puddled reflection of streetlamps. I was put in mind of a memory from eighth grade, a few weeks after my parents had separated. I'd been home on a winter's Saturday afternoon, and a violent thunderstorm had erupted out of nowhere then, after a minute or two, stopped just as suddenly. I went out to our front yard, my sneakers squelching in the muck. A damp wind made our tall elm tree creak under the pewter sky. There were no people or cars out; if not for the houses around me, I could have been in a forest. Something about the moment — likely my adolescent conviction that my pain had more beauty, more holiness, than the average person's, that it was exceptional and exquisite — compelled me to tell myself to memorialize it. I suppose it is this kind of egotistical delusion that drives some people to make art.

Remember this, I commanded myself again, though I knew that this memory — like all of them — would lose an essential and truthful quality over the years. The notion that we repress or redact significant chunks of the past strikes me as a dramatic contrivance for storytellers more than a realistic psychological phenomenon; but that we alter our retrospection in subtle ways, to airbrush out unpalatable blemishes here and there, much as we sweep detritus in our present consciousness under the carpet: that seems quite natural.

I waited until the next Monday, when Billy was out, to call my father at his office.

"I thought we agreed on a budget," he said.

"I'm really sorry," I said. "I didn't realize how expensive my books would be this semester."

He had the income that enabled him to accommodate my request, but not without a sigh. "I'll put a check in the mail today."

"I'll watch my spending more carefully," I promised and hung up more ashamed than I normally was after soliciting him for money.

When I went to the bathroom, I noticed that the grayish film in the tub I had once been accustomed to was making a comeback. Not only had Billy neglected to clean the day before, I realized, but he hadn't done it the previous week, either. When he returned in the afternoon from his classes, he was wearing a pair of Levi's 501s and Adidas Sambas I hadn't seen on him before. "I'm going to Gristedes," I told him at his desk. "Do you need me to pick up any cleaning supplies?"

"I think we're good," he said.

"Okay. Because the bathroom's looking a little scummy."

"Yeah, sorry, I was too hung over to clean it yesterday. I've got work in a few hours, but I'll get to it tomorrow."

"Thanks." I started toward my room but stopped; he was pretending it was just a day late when it was really a week overdue. "It'd be great if you could do it sooner rather than later. I'm not asking for any contributions from you other than you clean."

He headed to the kitchen. "Of course, man. You're right."

"You can do it later," I backtracked. "Tomorrow's fine. It's not a big deal."

"I'll do it now," he insisted. He breezed past me to gather the supplies. Normally that was my cue to leave the apartment, but that day I shut myself in my room. A couple of hours later I heard his footsteps in the hall and expected him to knock on my door and tell me he was moving out. But of course he didn't. He couldn't. He was stuck with me.

Instead the front door thumped closed, and I went out to the living room. He'd left the entire place as immaculate as the first time he'd cleaned. A plate with a chicken breast, steamed broccoli, and rice serenely awaited me on the table. A folded cloth napkin, silverware, and an unlit candle completed the hostile presentation.

On an afternoon walk through the East Village I heard my name. It was Oliver, an NYU classmate with whom I had a number of friends in common. I hadn't seen him since grad school began, and we caught up briefly before he had to get back to work.

"See you in Maine this summer, if not

before?" he said before departing.

"Maine?"

"Peter's wedding."

"I don't think I even knew he had a girlfriend," I said.

Oliver looked sheepish. "It was kind of a whirlwind romance," he said. "And they're putting people up in houses, so it's a pretty small wedding. It's gonna be such a pain in the ass, driving all the way up there July Fourth weekend."

"Send him my best," I said. "And say hello to the others for me."

Adam's story ran in the *Atlantic Monthly*, and, going by the chatter at school, you would think he'd scored a Pulitzer. The other students deemed it worthy of the magazine, though I assumed this was from either politeness or being hoodwinked by its prestigious home.

I was reluctant to give Adam the unwitting satisfaction of my spending voluntary time with his prose, especially since "Camp Redwood" had been published around the same time to no fanfare. But when I planted one of my contributor copies in the center of the bookshelf of literary journals in the library, the glossy cover of the *Atlantic Monthly* taunted me from the more imposing periodicals shelf. I needed to read it, to confirm that it was a sham.

The story wasn't as bad as I'd remembered it; the humor was understated, the prose sharp, the characters engaging. Halfway through I nearly forgot who the author was, and by the end I had to begrudgingly concede: Adam had produced a strong piece of fiction, and I was more upset to find out that he'd succeeded through merit, not fraudulence.

When I replaced the magazine in a corner of the rack, with a cholesterol medication ad on the back cover facing out, I had the even more painful realization that his *Atlantic Monthly* issue, one of hundreds of thousands circulating throughout the country, would likely survive as long as the printed word did, Adam's creative output and the cholesterol medication both archived and immortalized, whereas, after not that many years, it would be almost impossible to locate a copy of my no-name literary journal.

I returned to the library a week later to check on the journal. It was still in the same spot, its spine uncracked.

It was an eighty-degree March day inspiring "If this is global warming, I'll take it" jokes.

I was on the downtown 9 after class when a knot of commuters pressed through the doors at Seventy-Second Street. The new passengers dispersed like heat-seeking missiles for available seats, and a man around my age sat to my left.

As I edged over to give him room, I noticed that his right arm terminated in a pinched knob of skin just beyond the hem of his T-shirt. With his left hand he turned the pages of a paperback on his lap. I tried to read my newspaper, but his arm was in my peripheral vision the entire time, and the nubby point kept calling my attention.

I hated myself for my discomfort then deflected my ire to the innocent man, who appeared completely at ease with his missing forearm, with no hang-ups about flaunting it in short sleeves.

My body remained rigid until Fourteenth Street, when I stood up before the train had fully stopped. I lost my balance and my hand brushed against his arm, which felt like the end of a pestle. A shock streaked up my arm, as if I'd touched electric fencing.

"Sorry," I muttered as I righted myself and plowed through the crowd, the sensation staying with me the rest of the day as if it were my own phantom limb.

9

A letter arrived in the first-years' mailboxes, and within hours all the MFAs were buzzing about it. A donor had given Columbia's graduate arts programs a large sum of money, and among the earmarked initiatives, the writing program would offer one rising second-year student from each genre a stipend of seven thousand dollars. To apply, prose writers had to submit, in a couple of weeks, fifty pages of work and a proposal outlining their writing plans for the fellowship year. Judgments would be rendered by all of the tenured faculty members.

I put it out of my mind, as I had no chance of winning. Billy, no doubt, would be a front-runner. Other students had strong reputations — Adam's stock had risen as a result of his *Atlantic Monthly* story — but none had impressed our professors as his work had, and he would certainly get a boost as a financially needy candidate.

"You applying for that fellowship?" I casually asked from the couch before he left that night to bartend. Since the cleaning episode, our interactions had been limited to logistics.

"Yeah," he said as he tugged on his Adidas. "You?"

"I don't think so. I don't really have a shot."

He nodded as though this were not worth even politely disputing. "Later," he said.

We'd had enough of each other. He'd stayed with me so long only out of desperation. With the stipend he'd have enough money to move out to a university-subsidized apartment. I hoped he would win it and be gone — a clean, natural ending to our friendship.

Matt and Adam were throwing a party that weekend. Billy didn't mention it to me, and I wasn't planning to go. Then the night rolled around and I had no plans. Annoyed that I was staying home so as not to impinge on his turf, I took the subway uptown.

Billy was in a corner of the living room with Adam, Matt, and the Super Bowl watchers. I joined a group far from them before glomming on to another when that one dissolved. I always hated this aspect of

228

a party, pinballing around and latching on to new clusters like a barnacle searching for a hull. Certain people — Billy was one — never needed to circulate in social spaces; with their gravitational pull of charisma, others orbited them.

My classmates carped about their workloads, gossiped about two young professors rumored to be an item, speculated on the unsolved murder of Biggie Smalls. Through the forest of partygoers' limbs, I allowed myself to look over at Billy holding court to a trio of girls. In his new jeans and sneakers and one of his threadbare T-shirts, you'd never know he was from a small town in Illinois, that half a year ago he'd been terrified to speak to a couple of women in a bar for fear of coming off like a rube. He looked like he belonged, as much as if not more than anyone else in the room. He looked like a New Yorker.

Someone passed around a joint. I hesitated when it reached my hand; though I held my liquor fairly well, my tolerance for marijuana was astonishingly low. In the right company, with the right strain of pot and mood, I turned extroverted, finding everything funny and interesting and wondrous, but one puff could also render me the sole inhabitant of a dark, distant planet.

I took a chance. The sweet helium toke burst within me, traveling straight from my lungs to my head, and when a guy said, "I've got two words to describe this weed: *a lot,*" everyone found his off-kilter summation and emphasis funny, and stoned giggles begat giggles. As a belly laugh unstoppered me, I felt the camaraderie of our collective stupor; though I hadn't gotten to know them well yet nor they me, we would someday, maybe next year, I'd been sinking my energy into Billy when it should have been with them, these were my people, the potential for human connection was always there, all it took was spending time with others and lowering your shield.

Then someone said of a poetry professor, "What's up with that weird birthmark on his neck?" and the rest began speculating on whether it was carcinogenic, if he could get it removed, how distracting it was in class, how the professor also had a throat-clearing tic they suspected was psychologically linked, and the *a lot* stoner said, "That guy's a classic oddball."

The switch flipped, and I retreated into the subterranean corridors of my mind with the thought that often came to me in sobriety, too: I would never relate to these people after all, they wouldn't come to know me and no one ever would, and it wasn't because I was a misunderstood rebel or suffered from some diagnosable pathology; I was an oddball — but not even a "classic" oddball, no, I was an oddball among self-selecting oddballs who had found community with other oddballs, and to be on the outside of mainstream society is one thing, an admirably heroic struggle, but to be on the fringes of an already marginalized subculture is simply lonely.

The only thing that helped me relax in these situations was more alcohol. I flattened myself sideways through the bodies in the hallway to reach the empty kitchen, where I had a shot of whiskey, felt a little calmer, and fixed another, nipping at it while clutching the bottle.

Billy swaggered into the kitchen, Adam and Matt in tow. "Hey," I said before they saw me and held up the whiskey. "Want some?"

"Thanks, dude," Adam said.

I poured a generous serving for each of them in silence.

"Look at that," said Billy. "You're the bartender now. Serving the masters of the house."

"Watch out or I'll take your job at the Eagle's Nest," I said.

Billy swallowed his drink then grabbed the bottle from me and sloshed some more into his cup. "Y'ever had one, though?" he slurred.

"Had what?"

"Have you actually *had* a job?" He articulated each syllable with emphasis.

"You know I have," I said. "I was a copy editor for two years before this."

His smile wasn't the inclusive, ingratiating one I was used to. "A real job. Not where you're fixing the commas in some fashion magazine."

"I haven't had any manual labor jobs, if that's what you're asking," I admitted.

He kept staring at me, his head swaying a little but his eyes fixed. It was unnerving.

"I'm just messing with you, dude," he finally said with a short laugh. "I know you haven't. You've got the softest fucking hands in the world."

Adam and Matt looked into their drinks. "We should get back out there," Matt said.

"Seriously," Billy persisted, "how do you get through life with your hands like that? It's like you haven't even fucking *typed*." He put down the bottle, collared my wrist, and held out my palm for inspection. "You've got to feel this. It's like a fucking baby's skin. Go on, touch it."

"All right," Matt said, slinging a placating arm around Billy's shoulders. "Let's get some food." He guided him out of the kitchen before he could say anything else. People moved aside, females and males alike drinking in his unassailable looks as he passed. How easily he could mock me for my privileges, but I doubted he had ever considered the copious ones he enjoyed, which society didn't catalog as overtly, the love and affection he knew would show up at his doorstep without fail, whereas I was in the starved ranks of those who had to grasp for it when it was within reach for fear of its slipping away. And he was never made to feel guilty for these natural advantages and resources he'd done nothing to earn. The rest of us just revered him for them — I most of all.

I gave Billy a wide berth the next few days, keeping to my room. When I came home from workshop that week, the door to the neighbor's apartment was propped open, "Macarena" filtering out to the hall from a radio. I paused by the threshold, afforded a rare view into her cloistered world, the fascination of glimpsing an identical blueprint to your home but with a completely different constitution.

233

Only there was nothing inside other than a crew of workmen and drop cloths. I stepped out of the path of one of them. "She moving out?" I asked.

"I think she died," he said.

It must have happened while Billy and I were on campus or we would have seen some evidence of her body's removal. I looked back into the emptied-out apartment. Decades of life contained within it one day — couches with worn upholstery and coffee tables with interlocking rings in the wood, fading photographs, books that hadn't been opened in years, tchotchkes with no organizing principle other than that they belonged to a specific person, the distinctive smell of one's home — and absolutely nothing the next. I couldn't remember her last name.

She deserved a drink in memoriam. In my apartment I poured a fist of liquor, plopped in an ice cube, and sat on the radiator with a cigarette to take in the sunset, which had burned the sky a demonic red. I'd have more evenings like this again — comfortably alone in my own space — once Billy moved out, assuming he won the fellowship. And he would win it. He won at everything: writing, women, friends. He may have come from a disadvantaged background, but everyone he encountered was eager to help him triumph over it, for one reason or another, and though he was ostensibly against government handouts, he had no reservations about benefiting from their largesse — or mine.

I found myself nursing my next drink at Billy's desk. The desktop took a few minutes to boot up, whirring and groaning like a decrepit car engine struggling to life. I poked around his hard drive until I found his fellowship proposal. Then I saw eight files named NOMANS, sequentially numbered, and opened the newest one, which had one hundred and eighteen pages.

How easy it would be, I mused, as I skimmed his beautiful novel and drank my whiskey, to destroy his chances to win.

In retrospect I would like to blame the alcohol. I clicked on page one hundred and twelve and scrolled up, the paragraphs darkening like a bleeding inkblot, until I'd selected ninety pages. Without them, he'd have only twenty-eight pages, well below the application requirement. He would attribute it to a mysterious computer glitch from his geriatric machine; he might not even notice the missing middle section and would save over it, obscuring any digital fingerprints of mine.

I pressed the Delete key and saved the file. I was about to turn off the computer when I recognized my obvious oversight: his older versions would be long enough for the application, too. I deleted corresponding ninety-page chunks from them along with those from their floppy disk backups. Only when I was done with the whole erasure did the foolishness of my plan register. It no longer looked like a computer bug; to be missing the same exact section from multiple files across different formats was a clear sign of human intervention, and I was the only other human with access to his computer. I reopened the newest version, thinking there might be a technical fix, but if one existed, it was beyond my comprehension.

Even worse, in the bottom drawer were the printouts of his workshop submissions and his longhand notebooks. All I'd done was force him to retype the missing pages, which he could easily accomplish in the week remaining before the application was due. I couldn't do it myself, since the hard copies were filled with line edits and he'd made further revisions on the computer; my tampering would be evident.

Perhaps because of my fixation on plotting, I'd long been uncomfortably aware of how little it would take to derail one's course in life — stepping off the curb a second too early, accidentally dropping someone's baby — and in my fears the outcome was always grisly or fatal. By comparison, deleting text from an unpublished novel was paltry, and yet, in the whiskey-soaked moment, the moral undertow felt just as catastrophic. Needing to cover my tracks, I paced the apartment in frenzied search of a solution.

By the window, I watched one of the workmen carting off my former neighbor's excavated double-basin sink on a dolly.

I called Oliver from NYU and invited him to join me for dinner in the East Village in an hour. "That's late," he said. "I was just about to order in."

"I'm celebrating almost finishing the semester," I told him. "My treat."

He succumbed when I suggested a trendy Italian restaurant at Ninth and First. After we hung up, I brought the furniture dolly out of the entryway closet and over to Billy's desk, unplugged his computer, and set it on the dolly. Then I stacked his file cabinet on the computer's chassis and the monitor and VCR on that. After stowing my laptop in my backpack and making sure no one was in the hallway, I rolled everything out to the elevator, exiting the building through the back entrance.

Dusk was encroaching. I steered the dolly east, passing a throng of luggage-wheeling Delta flight attendants, none of whom gave me a second look, propelled by momentum and thoughts of how Billy had reveled in my humiliation at the party. Once I crossed the FDR Drive, I headed south along the pedestrian walkway to the semi-secluded spot by the chain-link fence where Billy and I had thrown our Snapple bottles.

The East River lapped against a barrier below, murky and briny. After setting the VCR and file cabinet on the ground, I picked up the computer. The fence was too high, and the chassis bulky and heavy enough, that I couldn't easily throw it over. The impediment of gravity made me question, for the first time, the sanity of what I was doing. But it was too late. I'd already gone too far. I had no choice.

I hoisted the computer above my head, took a short running start, and heaved with everything I had. The computer arced over the fence like a high jumper barely clearing the bar. I had anticipated a violently climactic splash, but the beige device plummeted into the water with unruffled calm and sank.

The file cabinet was too full to lift overhead with all its contents intact. I cleaned out the top drawer, which contained only the floppy disk backups. The second drawer held pens, paper clips, a stapler, all easy to jettison.

It was the large bottom drawer that made up the bulk of the weight. I started with the pocket notepads, the inklings of ideas, and moved on to the notebooks, where they had transformed into complete, strung-together sentences. Next I grabbed a sheaf of duplicated printouts, his most recent submission to workshop, and chucked them over. They separated into their discrete stapled and paper-clipped units and fluttered apart, a slicing snowstorm of papers. Then another, and another, and another, until the drawer was empty and I could shot-put it into the river.

After that, I flung the VCR and the monitor and my laptop over the fence. I had recent backups on disk, but my work was disposable anyway, text that would stick in a reader's mind as ephemerally as graffiti on a passing subway car. No great loss; maybe even a gain. Sometimes the only way to start over in life is to burn down the house.

I raced back to the apartment, where I unseated the couch cushions, skewed my mattress off the bed frame, and rifled through the drawers of my bureau and leather-topped desk. After disarranging Billy's room and the entryway closet, I considered knocking a few glass bottles off their shelves but decided it would be over-kill. I was about to leave when I had the sensation that I was forgetting something crucial, and then I realized that there were no signs of a break-in on the door itself. Some mark had to be left behind, so I pulled out the hammer from Billy's tool kit. When the hallway was clear, I chipped the doorframe just enough for it to pass as forc-ible entry. With schoolwork in my backpack, I sprinted to the Italian restaurant.

"I'll have a beer," I said to the waiter as soon as Oliver and I were seated.

I finished my pasta in record time and requested the check when our entrées were cleared. "Want to grab a drink at my room-mate's bar down the block?" I asked as I paid and overtipped in cash.

"I'm exhausted," he said.

"One drink won't hurt you. It's on me still."

"I have a work thing in the morning."

"Please," I said. "I'm a little lonely."

Oliver looked flustered. We didn't have that kind of relationship. I didn't have that kind of relationship with anyone.

"I could do one drink," he said.

The Eagle's Nest was bustling, Billy yukking it up with a regular. He always looked natural behind the bar, more so than I felt on the other side of it. He seemed surprised by my appearance; I hadn't been to his workplace since the time I'd ambushed him with his friends.

"This is my friend Oliver," I said when Billy came for our orders. As he mixed our gin and tonics, I mentioned, as offhandedly as possible, "We just had dinner at that Italian place down the block. Pretty good."

Oliver left after his drink, but I stuck around. Billy was busy enough that we didn't have much time to talk, or, rather, much opportunity to be forced to pretend we had anything to talk about. Even if we'd been on better terms, even if I hadn't just obliterated all his work, I wouldn't have felt like discussing the neighbor with him. I switched to beer as I read for my classes, trying not to think about what I'd done. At one in the morning, with just the stragglers left, I ordered another.

"Don't you have class tomorrow?" Billy asked.

"Who cares," I said.

He popped off the bottle cap and cleared some crumpled napkins off the counter.

"Sorry I was kind of a dick last weekend," he said. "I drank too much."

"That's okay," I told him.

"No, it was messed up," he said. "I'm really sorry."

I nodded, though I hadn't wanted him to apologize, to mitigate the acid aftertaste from the party.

Someone called out for a drink. With another three hours until closing time, I decided to take a nap in one of the booths, and when I woke up the lights were on.

"Don't have to go home but you can't stay here," Billy said. I blinked as he went over to the old-timer in the tweed cap, also dozing in a booth. "Mr. Williams," Billy said, gently rousing him. "Mr. Williams, we're closing."

Mr. Williams slowly opened his eyes and spread the wings of his mustache with a close-lipped smile. I'd seen him every time I'd been to the bar, but he always kept to himself, so we'd never spoken or even acknowledged each other. But as he shuffled by, he tipped his head at me, a small salute of night-owl fraternity. I nodded back and suddenly regretted not engaging him before.

It had been a while since Billy and I had walked home together late at night, when we'd had the streets to ourselves, claiming deserted First Avenue like conquerors of the city and the evening. That night we didn't have much to say.

"I forgot how long your shifts are," I said.

"How many drinks you have?" he asked.

"I don't know. Six, maybe seven."

His chuckle nearly helped me forget what was awaiting us in the apartment, made me think the past several hours — the past several months — had never happened.

"Kind of stupid of me," I said. "I'll be paying for it tomorrow."

We reached our building and took the elevator. Though lucid, I'd had enough to drink that I felt at a remove from myself, as though I were watching a movie of someone else's life, especially when Billy opened the door and turned on the lights.

"What the fuck?" he said, looking at the couch cushions on the floor.

He went into his room. "Shit," he said. He moved to the bathroom and yanked the shower curtain to the side before going to my room and inspecting the closet. After checking the entryway closet and ensuring there were no intruders, he finally noticed what he'd overlooked in his initial alarm.

"Shit," he said again.

He crouched under his desk. Not finding his missing computer, he struck a fist against the desk.

"Fuck me," he said. He sat on his chair, raked his fingers through his hair, and rubbed his closed eyes with the base of his palms.

I felt a self-incriminating impulse to smile and bit my lip hard. "Goddamn it," I said when I went into my room. "My computer's gone." I returned to the living room. "And the VCR. Not the TV, at least."

Billy opened his eyes and looked over the side of his desk.

"Motherfuckers!" he said.

"What?"

"My file cabinet's gone." He shoved his desk, but it was abutting the wall.

"Was there anything valuable in it?"

"Just my fucking novel," he said.

"What else?"

"Nothing."

"That's weird," I said. "You have backups, right?"

"They were all inside it."

"I'll see if there's anything in the stairwell or the back lobby," I said. "Maybe they ditched our stuff."

I walked downstairs, as much to escape as for the illusion of due diligence. When I returned, he was still at his desk, head in hands. "Nothing," I told him. "Do other

244

people in the program have copies of your novel? Any professors?"

He perked up optimistically before his face darkened again. "No. Anyone who had parts of it gave it back to me."

I started to feel not only my growing remorse but his grief and tried to think of something to comfort him. "Didn't Hemingway's wife lose all his writing on the train?"

He didn't respond but searched under the couch and in the kitchen for anything that might have been left behind then examined the front door. He tapped the part of the doorframe that I'd chipped with the hammer.

"This wasn't like this before, was it?" he asked. I shrugged. "They broke in," he said. "If we file a police report, maybe there've been other robberies like this and they'll be able to track down the thieves, or they'll know if they're selling things to a pawn shop. Or maybe someone in the building saw something."

"We can't go to the cops," I said. "We're not even supposed to be here. And there's no way they'd ever look for our computers anyway. That's small potatoes to them."

"Well, fuck," he said. "So that's it? Everything's gone?"

"I don't know what to say," I told him. "This sucks. I'm really sorry."

A few minutes after I retreated to my room, thinking the episode was behind me, he was at my door.

"What about the insurance?"

"What insurance?"

"The renter's insurance," he said. "Your great-aunt renewed it, right? Can't we at least get reimbursed for our computers through that?"

That was what I'd forgotten.

"Only if it were actually her stuff," I said. "But you can't just say you had a computer stolen. She'd have to have listed a computer as a possession."

"Did she own a computer?"

When I'd moved into her apartment, among other items she hadn't yet transported to her New Jersey home was a seldom-used computer she kept in a corner of the bedroom. I recalled this only because its appearance in an elderly woman's home in 1990 had surprised me, and we'd discussed it; her son in Oregon had bought it for her after reading an article about senior citizens keeping their faculties sharp by using personal computers.

"I don't know," I said. "But even if she did, you need proof it was still around."

He rushed into his room, and I heard the scrape of his nightstand drawer. "This photo," he said as he returned, holding up the Polaroid I'd taken of him typing on his computer. The photo did capture the computer, the monitor, and what was recognizably the wall to our apartment. It might well stand up as a piece of evidence.

"Assuming she owned a computer, and kept it listed as property once she moved, they could tell it's not the same as this one," I countered.

"You can barely make out the computer," he said. He was right; it was out of focus, and the overall fuzzy picture quality made it even less distinct. "We have the other Polaroid, too."

"If the only pictures we have are of you using it, they might think it's yours and not hers and they won't reimburse us."

"So we say I'm her grandson and I was using her computer when she took them." His nostrils flared. "Come on, man! This is our only recourse. I can't afford a new computer, and I just lost two fucking years of work."

"I'll buy you a new computer," I offered. "This wouldn't have happened if you didn't live here."

"It's not your fault," he said. "And you've

247

already let me live here for free, and you've got to replace yours, too. Let's just try to file the insurance claim. Okay?"

This was all he had, and he wasn't going to let it go.

"Okay," I surrendered.

I hoped Billy might calm down by the next morning and accept my money for his computer, but as soon as I was up he asked me to call my great-aunt. He listened in by my side as I informed her about the supposed break-in.

Yes, she told me, she hadn't revised her inventory after she'd moved, so her (once-expensive) computer would still be listed, and its receipt had been documented with the insurance company. She'd owned a VCR, too.

"But if you think it's risky to file a claim, we don't have to," I said, to Billy's look of displeasure.

"Let me call them to see what they'd do," she said. "But you said you can't make out the computer in the picture? The bottom line is the apartment was broken into, and you deserve some reimbursement. It doesn't really matter which computer was stolen."

After she called the insurance company, she reported back that they needed her to contact the police first. Once that was done, it would take them four to six weeks to settle the claim.

"Aren't you concerned Stuy Town will find out about this?" I asked.

"They assured me Stuy Town won't get involved at all," she said. "It's just between the insurance people and the police."

She got in touch with our local precinct, who told her that her great-nephew could file the report in person. My plan was to downplay the burglary, letting the police know I didn't expect anything to come from reporting it in hopes of staving off an investigation.

"I think it should be me," said Billy. "I'm in the pictures. It'll sound fishy to say that you happened to have a photo of your friend using your great-aunt's computer."

"Then we'll use the photos of me," I said.

"You have a laptop computer," he said. "Your aunt had a desktop."

I lost the argument. Billy went to the police station a few blocks away and was able to get an officer to visit the apartment that afternoon. I made myself scarce during the inspection. When I returned a few hours later, Billy was on his bed, a notebook on his thighs. "So what happened?" I asked.

"The cop took a few pictures of the apartment," he said, scrawling in his notebook. "And he took the Polaroids with him."

"That's it?"

"He asked a few questions."

"Like what?"

"I don't know," Billy said. "He thought it was strange they took my file cabinet."

"Me too," I said. "Maybe they thought there was stuff they could take for identity theft or something. So what's the next step?"

"He said he'll be in touch in a few weeks." He clicked his pen twice. "You mind if we discuss this later? Trying to write a paper."

"I'm sure you'll get reimbursed," I said. "Probably for a lot more than your computer was worth."

He didn't say anything. I closed the door.

I shamefacedly asked my father for the money to buy a (cheaper) replacement laptop. He agreed, provided I started double-locking my door.

I went to class, I read, I attended school events. Life was back to normal.

A letter addressed to me, care of Columbia, came from a literary agent expressing his admiration for "Camp Redwood."

"Have you considered turning this into a novel?" he wrote. "I'd be interested in following these characters for another few hundred pages." I giddily shared the news with my parents and Billy.

"That's wonderful!" my mother effused.

"Terrific," said my father. "I just read an article about how big book deals are nowadays."

"Cool," Billy told me.

Encouraged by the agent, I decided I'd spend the summer and next year doing as he suggested and daydreamed about giving a reading from my future published novel at Columbia in front of Sylvia and Stockton without thanking them.

A couple of weeks later, the first-year students received another letter:

After reviewing dozens of applications to the second-year fellowships, we regret that we are unable to provide funding for all the strong work on offer. Upon careful consideration, we have awarded the fellowships to the following students: in poetry, Krista Evans; in fiction, Billy Campbell . . .

I felt, with an irony that registered even then, deceived.

I was bewildered as to how he'd even applied. The application required fifty pages; it was difficult to *type* that much in a week, not to mention write something of merit, no matter if it was fresh in his memory. He must have told Sylvia and Stockton about his work being stolen, and they'd given him the fellowship because they'd been planning on doing it anyway — the application had been a formality.

He was reading *Infinite Jest* when I came home. "Congratulations," I said; I was never that good at faking enthusiasm. "I heard about the fellowship."

"Thanks."

"How'd you rewrite all of it in a week?" As soon as I asked I feared that I sounded suspicious about his winning, that he knew I knew the professors had cut him a break.

"I didn't," he said. "This book agent reached out to me a couple months ago. She'd read some of my novel and liked what she saw and said I should send her the rest when I was done. I kind of put it out of my mind until I remembered she had the last copy. It was almost fifty pages."

So our professors hadn't simply handed him the fellowship, but they'd done him even better: they had recommended him to one of their agents. Even in the midst of misfortune he had good luck.

"Shit," I said. "That's great — that you got an agent, too. Why didn't you say anything at the time?"

"It wasn't an official offer or anything. And I thought it was maybe a prank. She said a book editor passed it along, but when I asked Stockton and Sylvia, they hadn't sent it to anyone."

"Oh." I twisted the doorknob back and forth. "It was me. I made a copy and sent it to my friend David Lankford last fall."

"Huh." He looked unsure of how to respond. "Well, thanks, man."

"So you going to quit the Eagle's Nest, now that you're loaded?" I asked, setting him up to tell me he was using his winnings to move out, too.

"Nah," he said. "Money's money."

10

The semester concluded uneventfully as final papers were submitted and faculty and students drank too much at end-of-year parties. Spring came later than expected, as always seemed to be the case in New York; the pear trees didn't reach full bloom until the first week of May. As the temperatures rose, office workers spilled outside during the lunch hour, sunning themselves like seals. The hard edges of the city were softened by new pockets of green, not least in Stuy Town, where the shouts of children echoed beyond the parameters of the courtyard. The renovation of the apartment next door was completed, and a young couple with a baby moved in.

"Even though I was the teacher, and you all were the students," Stockton said at the conclusion of our last class, with a mischievous smirk that gave away that this, too, was the setup to a much-employed punch line,

"I believe that, in the end, no one really learned anything."

Now that he had the means to afford rent elsewhere, I had expected Billy would tell me he was leaving. But apparently I had underestimated his Midwestern prudence; he made no mention of moving out. Things between us obviously weren't what they once were, but our ledger was somewhat clean — he'd recovered much of his novel, he'd won the fellowship, and I'd give him all the money once we received payment on the insurance claim — and I held out a modicum of hope for a partial reconciliation the next school year.

I called the Chinese place for lunch one afternoon and didn't get an answer. When I went down in person, I found that the restaurant had closed — permanently. A sign on the shuttered storefront indicated a bank branch would be taking its place. The food hadn't been that good, but the restaurant was inexpensive and open late, and its ketchup-colored awning, whenever I walked past it from the L train, was a reassuring reminder that things rarely changed in my sleepy neighborhood.

I went to Ess-a-Bagel instead and brought the mail in. Over lunch I read that week's *New Yorker* story — it was, I deduced in part from the abrupt opening and abrupter ending, the novel excerpt I'd overheard the editor talking up at the *Open City* party — then opened what I thought was the June rent bill. But it turned out to be a letter from Stuy Town consisting of one short paragraph:

Metropolitan Life Insurance Company [the owners of Stuyvesant Town], Landlords, hereby give [the name of my great-aunt], and all other occupants holding under them, twenty (20) days' notice to vacate the rental unit located at the above address. We have determined that the unit is not the tenant's primary place of residence, in contravention of the lease. A letter from our legal representation will follow.

I knocked on Billy's door. He was on his bed, typing on the used laptop he'd bought. I handed him the letter, which he read without saying anything.

"They're evicting us," I explained.

He nodded soberly.

"It might be a mistake," I said. "I'll call them."

I picked up the cordless phone, dialed the number on the letterhead, and reached a man in the lease department. After claiming I was calling on behalf of my great-aunt, who was too sick to use the phone, I asked for an explanation of the letter.

"Hold on, let me check . . . It says here that we were informed by the police of the presence of illegal tenants in the unit," he said with the bored sigh of a functionary whose life is not affected one iota by the devastating news he's imparting.

I told him that the police might have speculated that I was there illegally after they investigated a recent burglary, since I (really Billy) had let them in for my great-aunt, but it was all a misunderstanding; they must have incorrectly thought I was claiming to be the sole tenant.

"I don't have other details, and my supervisor is out of the office today," he said. "If you want more information, I suggest you ask the police."

"They say the police told them there was an illegal sublet," I said to Billy after I hung up. "The cop didn't ask who lived here, did he?"

He shook his head.

"I'm sure I didn't leave anything out that would make him think we were here illegally," I said. "I'm phoning the station now to clear this up."

"You sure this is worth fighting?" he asked.

"Are you kidding? Maybe not the insurance case, but I'm not just letting the apartment go like that. Especially not when I'm two fucking weeks away from getting it legally." He looked blank, and I reminded him of how, in June, I would be able to establish a year of cohabitation with my great-aunt via the phone bill and transfer the lease to my name.

I found the number for the Thirteenth Precinct in the Yellow Pages. They bounced me around to a few people before I reached a woman who had access to our report.

"It says the officer reported illegal tenants," she told me.

"I understand, but he can't just make a baseless charge like that," I said. "My great-aunt pays the rent and I pay the phone bill. We're both here legally."

"Sir, this is all the information I can release to you over the phone. I suggest you come down to the station and discuss it with the officer who filed the report. He's here today."

"You have to talk to the officer at the station," I told Billy after I hung up. "Worse comes to worst, we tell my great-aunt you've been living here with me and the picture was of you, so that's why we had you pretend to be her relative."

"This sounds really complicated," he said. "I can't keep all your stories straight."

"It's not. It's simple. We're in the right. She's legally permitted to have someone live with her as long as she's here, too."

"But she *doesn't* live here."

"They don't know that," I said. "You'll just ask the cop why he said there were illegal tenants. I don't even know why he'd care about that or why he'd say anything to Stuy Town — it's not his business. Did he seem suspicious while he was here? Did he look through my stuff or go through the mail, anything like that?"

He threw up his hands.

"C'mon, Billy, *think.* This is important. I'm calling a lawyer after this. We need to anticipate what their case is."

"Look, man. They're obviously intent on kicking you out," he said. "You don't want to get involved in some expensive legal battle you're bound to lose. It's just an apartment."

" '*Just* an apartment'?" His air of resignation was infuriating. He was losing out on the apartment for maybe one more year; I was losing it for decades. "You're not from here — you have no idea how valuable this is. New Yorkers would give a limb to get a rent-stabilized apartment for life."

Billy looked at me queerly.

"You really want to spend your whole *life* here?" he asked. "In this apartment?"

"It's worth paying for a lawyer," I said. "You don't just drop it because a cop has a hunch."

I flipped through the Yellow Pages for lawyers.

"I told him I lived here illegally," Billy said.

"You told him *what*?"

"That I was here illegally."

I felt a flush of anger.

"Why would you do that?"

"Because" — Billy hesitated — "he said there were a lot of insurance scams going on, and he accused me of one and said he could charge me with falsely reporting a crime. I told him I'd never pull something like that because I was just staying here for free and I wasn't the legal tenant. I thought that would convince him I was telling him the truth. I didn't think he'd tell Stuy Town."

The heat was spreading to other parts of my body like a rash. "Did he end up charging you?"

"No, he dropped it after that," he said.

"Good," I said. "That's good. So we'll pretend it was me, and I'll tell Stuy Town

260

that I've been staying here with my great-aunt, so when the cop threatened to charge me, I got scared and said I wasn't the legal tenant. Then in two weeks I'll show them the phone bill in my name, and I'll still be able to take over the lease." I exhaled a tense breath. "See? This isn't that complicated."

The phone in the crook of my neck, I returned to the Yellow Pages.

"Stuy Town and the police both said illegal te*nants,*" I said to Billy. "Plural. Do they think *two* of us live here?"

He looked down at his laptop screen.

"Shit," I said. "Okay, we have to come up with another excuse for that. We could say one of us was just crashing here for a few weeks. Did you tell him I live here, or did he just guess you had a roommate?"

He paused for several seconds — I thought so he could recall the incident.

"After I told him it wasn't a scam, the cop showed me the doorframe," Billy said. "He said the damage could only have been made when the door was already open, not from someone busting it open. And he said it looked like the person had hit it with something like a hammer to make it look like a break-in."

I could smell my sweat, the shameful sour tang of it.

"The cop is clearly wrong," I said. "It's New York City. Robberies happen all the time."

"The cop didn't dispute that a robbery happened," Billy said. "He said this one looked staged."

He stared at me with an expression that was all the more menacing for its composure.

"Why'd you do it?" he asked.

"What?" I said.

"Why'd you do it?" he repeated.

I made my face some amalgam of incredulous and indignant. "You think *I* did it? I lost my computer, too, remember?"

He continued to look at me with an unsettling calm.

"How could I have even possibly done it?" I said. "I was at dinner with my friend Oliver that night, then I went to the Eagle's Nest. It happened while we —"

"All my fucking work, man," Billy said with such definitiveness, such disgust, that I knew there was no point in continuing the charade. "Everything I'd written. All of it."

I shouldn't have faked the burglary. I shouldn't have deleted his work, shouldn't have gone on that wedding trip, shouldn't have invited him to move in with me in the first place. I should have kept living alone.

262

He would have left Columbia after a semester. I'd vaguely recall him as a classmate I knew briefly whose work I admired, and he wouldn't remember me at all. I would have kept the apartment forever, and my little world would have remained undisturbed. That was an easier way to go through life — on the margins, more observer than participant.

My eyes veered away to the photo of the union representative on the wall.

"You can't even give me a fucking answer," Billy said. "Were you jealous of me or something? You didn't even apply to the fellowship. You just didn't want me to win it? You're that competitive?"

The street sounds of a weekday afternoon — honking cars, the percussive blast of jackhammers, the Doppler effect of a wailing ambulance — floated up to our open windows.

"You know what that meant, to lose all that?" he asked. "I don't have a dad who pays for everything. This" — he tapped his laptop — "is all I have, man. It's the only thing I've got that gives me a chance not to be a bartender the rest of my life." His body was still, but his chest visibly expanded and contracted. "You know the only reason I didn't beat the shit out of you?"

He expelled a short, sharp laugh.

"Because I feel fucking sorry for you," he said.

I thought my skin had thickened from two semesters of relentless criticism in class, but these words, with their lack of specificity as to what he pitied in me, gouged deeper than any indictment of my writing ever could. My throat constricted. I blinked rapidly. He'd given me an out; I could claim pettiness, that I was competitive, I was jealous, and if I wasn't going to win, then I hadn't wanted him to, either.

But the real reason was more pathetic.

"I didn't want you to leave me," I said.

We were quiet again.

Maybe I wasn't telling him anything he didn't already suspect, or know, and I was really just confessing to myself what I'd been holding in all year: that Billy had activated something inside me no one else ever had, something that didn't fit into a neatly defined slot, that I couldn't quite bring myself to articulate. Though I suppose each experience like this, just like everyone's loneliness, feels uniquely uncategorizable — the particular contours of another person's borders that collide with your own before leaving behind a crater that will be there the rest of your life.

The garbage chute in the hallway swung shut with a bang as someone tossed out their trash.

"Jesus Christ," Billy said. "Stop fucking crying."

"I'm sorry," I said.

I wanted to apologize again but didn't know what else to say. I did have one question, though, a variation of what I'd asked him eight months earlier that had started all of this, only this time I had nothing to offer him. I already knew the answer, but I guess I needed to hear it from him.

"Do you want to look for another apartment with me?"

"I already made plans to get a place with Adam and Matt," he said firmly. "I'm moving out at the end of the month."

"You don't have to," I pleaded. "I'll pay the rent again."

"Sorry," said Billy, more softly this time.

I almost wished he'd maintained his harsh tone, so I could pretend to myself — I was good at that — that I wouldn't want to be with him anyway, that I preferred to be on my own. But I knew I'd lost him, for good, and as I stood in his doorway, the phone book in my hand suddenly heavy as an anchor, I had the premonition that, despite my youth, despite the endlessly refillable reservoir of the human heart, my carapace would grow its most impenetrable layer yet, and Billy would be the last person I'd come close to letting in.

"I understand," I said.

11

That night, Billy packed his laptop and a duffel bag of clothes and told me he was going to stay on Adam and Matt's couch until they all moved into a new place in June.

I let my parents and great-aunt know that the subletting jig was finally up, claiming I'd simply been caught by management, probably tipped off by a meddlesome neighbor. No one seemed that shocked or upset over this half-truth; if anything, they felt bad for me.

After his confession on my behalf, Billy had persuaded the police officer not to file charges against either of us. He did, however, inform the insurance company of what we'd done. Three days after Billy moved out, a letter arrived penalizing my great-aunt thousands of dollars for the fraud.

There was no way to hide that from her. I appropriated the police officer's theory and told them all that I'd pulled the insurance scam for the money. My parents were furious with my bogus explanation, even after I assured them that I hadn't done it to feed a drug problem.

"You could have just asked your father for more money," my mother said.

"How could you be so stupid?" was the reaction of my father, who hadn't raised his voice with me since childhood. After he thought it over, he told me he would cover the penalty but expected me to reimburse him.

"I've also decided that I won't pay your tuition for next year," he said. "Your mother thinks it's the right decision as well."

"I agree," I said.

I could have taken out a student loan, but tens of thousands of dollars in debt without the cushion of the Stuy Town apartment spelled years of immiseration. I notified Columbia that I would be taking an undetermined leave of absence in the fall.

I hunted for a budget apartment and found a fifth-floor walk-up in Murray Hill with three roommates. To help with the first month's rent, I called Steve, the copy chief of the men's magazine where I had freelanced, who said he needed another set of eyes for the current issue.

Billy and I hadn't spoken since he'd gone, so I asked Matt to tell him I was moving out the first of June, and he left a message on my machine letting me know he would retrieve the rest of his stuff that morning.

As planned, Billy returned to the apartment my last day there. I'd left the front door ajar and avoided him in my room, packing up as he cleaned his out. I hoped he would just leave without saying anything, but there was a knock and I told him to come in. He opened the door but stayed in the hallway, his duffel bag over a shoulder and two suitcases in his hands.

"Hey, man," he said. "I left my keys by the door."

I taped up a box. "Okay."

He looked back at the living room. "I don't need the desk or anything. New place comes furnished."

I nodded.

"Cool," he said. "Well, see you in the fall."

"Actually, I'm taking a leave of absence to go back to work," I told him. "My dad won't pay my tuition anymore, and I don't want to take out a student loan."

"Sorry to hear that," he said. "But it's probably a good idea, not taking on debt."

He walked away. After a step he pivoted back around.

"You know, getting out of this apartment might be a good thing," he said. "For both of us."

By "both of us" he meant me alone. I was the one who needed to be ejected from my cocoon, not he who had survived without one his entire life.

"Because it builds character?" I asked.

The chipped-tooth, tragicomic smile I'd seen so many times appeared — fleetingly, with less behind it, but still a farewell more generous than I deserved.

Then he closed the front door gently behind him and was gone.

A few hours later the movers arrived and began hauling furniture to their truck. They abandoned Billy's desk and everything else I wasn't taking on the street for scavengers or the sanitation department. They were done in half an hour.

Before I joined the movers at my new place, I stood at the front door, surveying the hairline cracks in the ceiling, the floor barred with shadows from the window partitions. I was caught off guard by the affection I felt seeing the apartment stripped to its bones, and though I knew it would be gut-renovated and there was no need to tidy up, I picked up a broom that had been left in the entryway closet and swept the living room floor.

Then I dug through my backpack for a pen and a scrap of paper, wrote "1990–1997" and my name, and dropped it into the slot in the medicine cabinet, where, along with the discarded and immured razor blades, I would like to think it remains.

■ ■ ■ ■

AFTER

■ ■ ■ ■

After some months of on-and-off work at the men's magazine, I proved a valuable enough asset to be hired full time under Steve and joined Manhattan's media-class army of ten-to-sixers. In addition to the principal, my father charged me interest on the insurance company penalty, and it took over a year of garnished paychecks to clear my debt.

I decided not to try to transfer to another MFA program — I had been rejected everywhere but Columbia the first time around and saw no reason why another application would yield a different outcome — but instead pinned all my hopes on the novel the literary agent had proposed I write. I worked on it nights and weekends, and three years later I sent it to him, with a reminder of who I was and a photocopy of the original "Camp Redwood" story from the literary magazine.

"Thank you for sending *Camp Redwood*," he wrote a few weeks later. "I read it with interest, and revisited the short story version, too. Unfortunately, I felt there was a brilliance and originality to the writing in the story that just didn't translate to the novel. I am sure others will feel differently, and I'll be cheering you on from the sidelines."

By that point I'd saved enough money that I could, with some belt tightening and part-time employment, afford my final year at Columbia. Given the opportunity, though, I had to acknowledge the truth I'd been deferring all that time: I wasn't meant to be a writer, and I wouldn't leave behind a novel, posthumously published or not.

Steve jumped to another magazine, and I was promoted to copy chief. I don't mind the work. I've always found a certain satisfaction in copyediting absent for me in writing. There are unambiguously right and wrong answers, rules to abide by, errors to remedy. I'm good; I go unnoticed. With my raise I rented a one-bedroom on a gentrifying street in Alphabet City, which I furnished with my own purchases. I'd never considered myself a cat person, but after seeing a kitten in a nearby lot three nights in a row, the next thing I knew I was buying tins of Fancy Feast and a scratching post.

I heard nothing from Billy and, not being in touch with anyone from Columbia, received no firsthand news about him. When he was twenty-nine he published *No Man's Land.* The only personal information on the book jacket was that he had earned his MFA from Columbia. I didn't go to any of his events and couldn't bring myself to read it. The novel was "warmly" received, meaning it didn't rocket him to literary fame and riches; what makes an MFA workshop salivate is usually greeted with benign indifference by the public. A collection of stories came out three years later, and his updated biography revealed that he was an associate professor at a college in Idaho. The jacket for his subsequent novel stated that he was now a professor at the same school and lived with his wife and children. More books, all set in the Midwest, followed at sporadic intervals. I continued not to read them — among other reasons, I was afraid of stumbling upon a character based on me — but their time-lapse author photos revealed him growing into the weathered handsomeness of one of his old T-shirts. He had become what he'd aspired to in his relatively modest field of dreams: a midlist writer with a tenured teaching job and a family.

My mother has grown close to Thomas's three children, who grew up nearby after he landed a job at Mass General, and sends me photos of them. As I predicted, my father retired to San Diego. We text on birthdays and holidays.

After a chimney collapsed almost a decade earlier, Chumley's has just reopened into an unrecognizable soigné establishment with wraparound leather banquettes and a burger whose black truffle supplement costs more than the dish alone. The Eagle's Nest closed years ago; in its location is a phone store. The ownership of Stuy Town has changed hands several times, and all new apartments are now deregulated, luxury-priced, and outfitted with stainless steel appliances, with the exception of a few units reserved for the winners of a housing lottery.

What social life I had after Columbia petered out as my peers married and had children. There was the occasional romantic encounter that might last a few weeks, but over time the succession of premature endings gradually depleted my morale, and my pursuits became fewer and further between. I didn't really notice my incremental retreat from people until it was nearly total. Sometimes I go to a bar by the office with my colleagues to toast the closing of an issue, listen to them talk about songs and celebrities I haven't heard of, and disappear after a drink, well before the karaoke and trivia contests begin. I've become the most senior employee; there are now college interns who were born after I started working there. I suspect they regard me with pity, a middle-aged bachelor with his elderly cat who inoffensively blends into the conference room walls at our Monday morning meetings. But solitude, I've discovered, isn't so bad once you come to expect it.

After the election returns came in, I stayed up for the immediate hand-wringing post-mortems analyzing how Democrats had brought this historic loss upon themselves, which were interrupted by the victory speech.

"The forgotten men and women of our country will be forgotten no longer," the president-elect vowed, to roars from his supporters.

I turned off the TV and sat in my dark living room. Then I went to the bedroom and rooted through the back of the closet for a box I hadn't opened in years. It contained everything I'd written at Columbia that Billy had edited. A set of jaundiced papers, they were the only remaining copies of my fiction; my digital files hadn't survived computer upgrades over the years, and at some point I'd thrown out my other classmates' and professors' feedback.

The papers were in reverse chronological order, starting with my workshop submissions in the spring; then "Camp Redwood"; a number of partial drafts from when we were still exchanging work informally in the fall; and, finally, the beginning of my abandoned novel.

I sat on the floor and read the entire chapter, including Billy's copious marginalia and editorial letter in his still-familiar handwriting with its unassuming precision.

The closet door creaked open a little, and I felt the static crackle of fur against my arm. "Sherwood," I said, setting down the papers. As I stroked the knobby ridge of his spine, beneath his chin, between his ears, his eyes rolled back and his jaw fell slack with contentment, the faint drumbeat of his heart pulsing behind his foreleg and driving blood through his delicate body.

"Don't listen to the others — this has enough 'emotional balls in the air,' whatever the hell that means," went the postscript Billy had written during class, on the backside of the final page. "And it's not 'flinching' either."

I hadn't remembered that last line — or maybe I'd stopped before reading it the first time.

I looked up at the mirror on the interior of the closet door and stared at myself for a long, unbroken time.

A paw between my shoulder blades.

"Still here," I said.

ACKNOWLEDGMENTS

I would like to thank the following people:

My wonderful editor and friend, Liese Mayer; her assistant, Grace McNamee, who contributed invaluable insights; my publicists, Lauren Hill and Emily Fisher; the production editor, Barbara Darko; the copy editor, Emily DeHuff, whose impeccable work has not gone unnoticed (all errors are mine); the proofreader, Missy Lacock; and everyone else at Bloomsbury.

My stalwart literary agent, Jim Rutman, and for his extra-literary agenting, Will Watkins.

My early readers, for their wisdom, encouragement, and forbearance: Sarah Bruni, Amber Dermont, Alena Graedon, Robert Kuhn, Steven Kurutz, Aryn Kyle, Diana Spechler, John Warner, and Piper Weiss. For answering my medical queries, Sherwin Zargaroff, MD.

Kate, who went through this again with

me, and so much else.

And lastly, Angus: this book was conceived, and a draft delivered, before you were, but your existence has since altered its pages profoundly — and more so its author. I hope you someday know how happy you've made me.

A NOTE ON THE AUTHOR

Teddy Wayne is the author of *Loner, The Love Song of Jonny Valentine,* and *Kapitoil.* He is the winner of a Whiting Writers' Award and an NEA Creative Writing Fellowship, as well as a finalist for the Young Lions Fiction Award, the PEN/Bingham Prize, and the Dayton Literary Peace Prize. A regular contributor to the *New Yorker,* the *New York Times,* and *McSweeney's,* he lives in Brooklyn with his wife, the writer Kate Greathead, and their son.

The employees of Thorndike Press hope you have enjoyed this Large Print book. All our Thorndike, Wheeler, and Kennebec Large Print titles are designed for easy reading, and all our books are made to last. Other Thorndike Press Large Print books are available at your library, through selected bookstores, or directly from us.

For information about titles, please call:
(800) 223-1244

or visit our website at:
gale.com/thorndike

To share your comments, please write:
Publisher
Thorndike Press
10 Water St., Suite 310
Waterville, ME 04901